ies

7

This book is to be returned on or before
the last date stamped below.

MIDLOTHIAN DISTRICT LIBRARY

Renewal may be made by personal application, by post
or by telephone.
If this book is lost or damaged a charge will be made.

The High Tide Talker

ELSPETH DAVIE

The High Tide Talker

AND OTHER STORIES

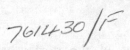

7614430/F

HAMISH HAMILTON
LONDON

First published in Great Britain 1976
by Hamish Hamilton Ltd
90 Great Russell Street London WC1B 3PT

Copyright © 1976 by Elspeth Davie

SBN 241 89446 8

Some of the stories have appeared in the
*Cornhill, Transatlantic Review, Gambit,
Penguin Book of Scottish Short Stories,
Signature Anthology* (Calder & Boyars),
Beyond the Words (Hutchinson) and *Scottish
Short Stories* (Collins).

The publisher acknowledges the financial assis-
tance of The Scottish Arts Council in the
publication of this volume.

Printed in Great Britain by
Northumberland Press Ltd, Gateshead
and bound by Richard Clay (The Chaucer Press) Ltd,
Bungay, Suffolk

To Anne

CONTENTS

A Lost Toy

Logan stood alone in the back garden of his house, listening for the approach of his neighbour from the other side. Any moment now she would be round. He heard from the next-door window the wailing of her child who had been put to bed. And he knew why the child wailed. Now he heard the bang of the gate, the determined feet. Mrs Kite was coming down the path towards him and an angry mother is a formidable sight. A forbidding woman at the best of times—her eyes were now a shade darker, her voice deeper. Forbidding, he thought, for want of a better word. But frightening was the better word. He stepped forward. 'Yes,' he said. 'Oh yes, Mrs Kite. I've searched the whole garden, dived under every bush. I'm sorry, but it just isn't there.'

'I'm very sorry too, but I'm afraid you'll have to look again. It *is* here. Angus won't sleep without it. And there's no doubt about it. Your boy had it last, and what's he done with it? Angus won't sleep!'

She held a finger up. As though obediently answering a summons the wailing started up again—a knowing wail, rhythmical, remorseless, searching out the hidden weaknesses of adults. Logan was not moved. What did move him to misery was the sight of his own son's head appearing from the dark square of the window above. This small head was held absolutely still for fear of being seen, while a wildly anxious wind ruffled the hair and flicked the thin black leaves of the tree outside into an agitated frame for his face. The child was not simply worried. He was afraid. Logan felt a terrible pang of concern for him and at the same time rage at the woman. Yet these feelings were out of all proportion to the event, and he knew it. He controlled his emotion.

'Look, I'll go through the whole place again. I'll rake through every blade of grass. I promise you, if it's here, I'll find it. But I can't go on after dark, can I? Do you want to help?'

She cast her eyes down to her shoes—cream shoes with polished buckles.

'No, I'm afraid I'm not wearing the right sort of thing.' She was not, he knew, referring to her shoes at all but to the great, unweeded darkness at the foot of his garden and the marshy smell of the wet bank beyond. She was making out that she stood on the edge of a primeval jungle.

'All right. I'll have one more look. After that we can call it a day.'

But it would soon be night. There was a yellow slit along the horizon, and though the tops of the trees still sparkled the long grass at their roots was beginning to hold a fringe of the dark. Logan moved deeper into the search. Puffy, withered roses brimming with the cold autumn rain which had fallen that morning sluiced water round his knees and thorns drew a red line on his wrist. He was aware of the woman still standing on the path behind, staring at him. If it's true that only a mother is a match for another woman, he thought—or come to that, any other baleful influence—then I've lost the game already. John has no mother. So how am I going to protect him from the harpies and the witches and the cunning ones in the shadow? Or how will I make him strong enough to take them all on? He was parting huge leaves with his hands, grovelling around thick wet stems. No plants he'd ever known before. These were monster weeds he'd never bothered about. The whole place was overgrown and uncared for. Was it indeed a jungle he'd allowed to grow up round about them? He remembered how his wife had cared for this garden. And it was she who'd looked after the child—one who needed care. Now more than ever. At times he worried himself sick, lying awake at night remembering the unexpected hollows behind the boy's ears when he turned his head, his laboured breathing under stress. And when, by the way, did he ever laugh? Would he himself manage to provide enough fatness and calm? He plunged deeper where the big trees stood close, bordered by prickly bushes where once there had been a trim hedge. He walked bending low to right and left. He remembered he was supposed to be searching for a toy.

The toy belonging to his neighbour's child was not a pleasant one. Logan had laughed when he first saw it to hide a faint disgust. This was one time his small son had laughed too—a bold laugh to hide what his father felt certain was a faint fear. It was a small brown bear. No doubt it had been sold like any other furry toy, to be cuddled. But something had gone slightly wrong in the making. Or the man or woman who'd made it had something else in mind, had remembered a certain viciousness in bears. Or in themselves. Had introduced a menace about the small, deeply-embedded pink eyes which had no doubt brought more than a touch of menace to their own as they sewed in the bits of dull red glass. They had even bothered

3

to put the authentic inturned claws on the beast, and to crown all, a thin, ugly patch on the fur where you could see right through to a patch of canvas skin, as though this bear had been bitten in some fight before it had even ventured onto the market world. The makers of such a toy had known the wrong bears. They had not been bed-time bears. They had perhaps heard the few bear stories from Canadian relatives which had not been bedtime tales. Once or twice, absently holding the animal in his hands, he himself had remembered one or two accounts which had found their way into British papers—that great, dim-sighted killer bear, for example, which had waited half the night outside a schoolboy's mountain camp and in the morning moved in to drag the smallest off. So much for this innocent teddy-bear and his makers who'd brought it to mind!

He prowled on, moving slowly down the steep slope of the garden and further into the hollow where there had once been a rockery. He and his wife had made it when they first moved in. Now it was nothing more than a stony place where you had to be careful not to twist your ankle coming down in the dark with an armful of garden refuse for the top-heavy dump. And lucky if on the way past the shed you didn't find the bin disgorging! Everything overflowed nowadays—bins, beds, tables and cupboards. His own impatience raged and flowed against himself for his inability to keep things going smoothly as before: and his anxiety flowed continually round the child. He couldn't name the anxiety though he longed to exorcize it. It sprang from a variety of things. From the hollows he sensed in the depths of the child as though the zestful marrow had been extracted from the bone when the mother died, from a daily dependence on himself mixed

4

with a remoteness his father couldn't reach, from his occasional nightmares, his visible strain with certain people —the Kites, above all, with their sharp-eyed questioning. Yet in an odd way his son was strong too. One day he might be very strong indeed. He had only to recognize this strength, have confidence in it, for his own doubts to subside and the boy's vague fears to vanish. He knew it. But how was it to be done?

He looked back once over his shoulder. The two figures were motionless, one in the square of the window, the other on the path and both watching him intently—one with trust, the other with dislike, he didn't care to think how deep. She would be only too glad if he never found the bear, if she could go on reproaching him for ever more over its loss. From a distance the wailing started, stopped and started again. He went on. Seeds snapped in the last warmth of the day. Floating leaves crisped down on his head. Sometimes, like an idle under-water swimmer, he stroked the space in front of him with both hands to disperse the criss-crossing of spiders webs which rose and fell, swung, broke, reknotted and floated before him, web against web, far into the distance in a scarcely discernible net of silver silk. He was near the water. It was a small pond, scummy with insects' wings and dead leaves—not much more than a waterlogged hollow which the rain made big in winter and the sun sucked dry again in summer. Beyond it was a little wood of rowans and thin, white birch trees fading back into the grey distance. He struggled through weeds to the water's edge, but no further. He stared down. Does she expect me to wade in up to my knees looking for the damned animal? To climb a tree to see if a bird has taken it up? Or to explore the holes in case a weasel has dragged it down? Does she want me to crawl on my hands and knees? He would look about him for two more minutes. Then he would turn.

The place where Logan stood was hidden from the house and the rest of the garden, hidden from all the other back windows. No sounds reached it. The spot seemed miles from the busy suburban road and the swish of family cars, and silent as it must have been long before there was a house in the place. Logan drew a deep breath and folded his arms. When they were first married and John was still a baby they had actually had picnics on the other side— had even planned to clear it a bit, bring the path round to the water's edge, cut down a tree or two and make it a shelter and a sun-trap. A sun-trap! Now you could scarcely see the sky. He could remember the baby sitting beside a large yellow basket trying to draw himself up to look over its rim, and at last rolling up his eyes, staring and grabbing at each packet which his mother drew out in a high curve over his head. Logan pictured this movement going on and on in an endless circle of summer—the round, sun-flecked heads of child and mother, the child's hand reaching up as more and more surprises were lifted out and put on the grass beside the round, calm pond. All this, he had once felt, could be contained forever within the circle of his own arms. Nothing could threaten it. Well, the circle had been violently broken—the woman dead, the child made vulnerable. For months the pond had been choked and darkened as though continually stirred in its depths.

Logan lifted his head, looked over the circle of water to the far bank, and saw an enormous brown bear. He saw no trees, no water, no colour of grass or sky, remembered nothing but embedded eyes, a great head poised as though blindly sniffing the air, a shoulder with a bitten patch.

6

The sight was sharp, cold, unshocking as a cut-out. But feeling, rushing upon the sight, was as instantaneously clear. The creature had no interest in *him*! In whom then? But I have only to keep my eyes on it for one instant—on this huge, unheard-of, unblinking, unbelievable block of brown non-bear. For one instant. He held it. Dropped his eyes to the pool. Looked again.

There was no bear. The bead-bright rowan berries circled a clear space, and in front untroubled wings, leaves and seeds sailed on the water. Nets of flies rose and fell on the still air. Not a sound yet from the windows or back gardens behind. The whole place awaited his first move. But he was very slow to move. For a long time he stood without turning his head, still looking down at the water, his hands clasped behind his back in an attitude which would have seemed casual to anyone who did not see his face. But at last he moved. He was turning himself slowly round on the spot, first away from the pond towards his house, then round again to the water and again towards the house and round again, making a full, spinning circle on the bank while his arms swung up to balance himself. The giddiness of his spin brought him at last to a stand-still, facing his own house. But he knew what he'd set in motion. The shattering break in the circle must somehow be joined—past with present and natural with super-natural, the garden with house and the hand stretching up with the down-reaching arm. Let these finally break apart—then brute and bully, nightmare and phantom would take over. 'And the bear must go!' he said aloud.

He started to move back again the way he'd come, climbing up till he'd almost reached the place where the vegetation cleared and he could see right up into his garden and along the line of back windows where one or two early lights were now showing. The rigid puppet-figure of his neighbour was still there on the path. The little boy was still at the window which was now shut. It came to Logan with a shock that he'd never noticed the unnatural stance of his son. From this distance he appeared rigid, fixed like a picture in a frame. No child should wait like this. Logan crashed up the last of the ridge, through reaching branches and spearing grass. He almost leapt into the garden brandishing his arms, defiantly empty. So what should he say to the woman now? No, Madam, I have *not* found your child's toy but if it's of any use to you I saw a killer bear behind the shrubbery. He ran forward waving and shouting to his son, trying to make him shout back. In fright or grief if need be. But shout he must.

'John!' he called. 'Open up!' The boy peered through the glass, put out his hand and slowly opened up a slit of the window. His lips moved. 'Oh *louder!*' called Logan. 'I can't hear you.' The little boy put his head out. 'Have you got it?' he called down in a thin voice.

'Got what?' Go on. Say it. He's *got* to say it.

'Bear,' the boy called down softly. The man laughed:

'No, and I'm not to bother either. Aren't we finished with that bear?'

'What's that?' came an angry voice from the path. He'd almost forgotten the woman there. He turned to her.

'Finished,' I said. 'We've done all we can.' It was getting darker now, with one or two stars, and the red planet was actually brightening up somewhere over her left shoulder. Mars, was it? So we're in for war. As though on command again the wailing started up from next door.

'No,' the woman was saying. 'No, I don't think you've done all you can, Mr Logan, and I suggest that before it's really dark ...'

'Look, Mrs Kite, tomorrow I'll produce any other toy you care to name. I'll take your boy with me and he can choose himself.'

'No use! This is the one. It's the one he wants—the one and only, and he's got to have it!' In her awful brooding rigidity she'd have liked to spread panic. But she was too late. Panic had already loomed and vanished.

'I've finished for the night,' he said again.

'Do you hear that crying?' she said, pointing. He heard it all right. But how much more he was concerned with the silence of his son.

'Do you know what *I* think?' she said, drawing near. 'I think your boy has got it. Up there.'

It was his turn to exclaim fiercely: 'What's that!'

'Yes. Up there. You wait and see. Well I can't stay here all night, can I? I've got to get back to poor Angus and try to get him to sleep somehow. But you're going to hear more of this. I'm not letting it drop. Don't think it!' She pivoted on her heel like a great dark doll and went purposefully back up the path. He heard the gate click and the steps going towards the house next door.

Logan looked up. John was not at the window. He had to whistle softly once or twice before, reluctantly, the child's head appeared again—a pale disc in the surrounding grey.

'Did you hear what she said, John?' his father asked. The head nodded.

'Well, what do you say to it?' There was silence above. But along the row of houses on either side, behind drawn curtains, the muted sounds of dozens of domestic evenings had begun—TV voices above the click of china, taps gushing into baths and sinks, hammering and singing and

9

nagging. But still a silence above. At last the voice came down:

'It's *not* me. I think *she* had it all the time!'

'What? Speak louder!'

'*She* found it and hid it when you were down there at the pond.'

'Watch it!' called his father. 'Be careful what you say.'

'I think she hid it under her coat!' The voice ended on a gasp.

The man below was silent. Behind the window next door—so near the one above there was only a brick or two between—there was a stirring. He imagined the two in there, not as mother and son, but as conspirators plotting. In a moment or two a head would look out, or perhaps both heads. He kept his eyes fixed on his child.

'Take care.' He spoke quickly. 'We can all see—imagine we see things.' He was now aware that a head did look out from the window next door, but whether mother or child he didn't know. He didn't look.

'I can see things that never happened,' he went on. 'And so can you. But when it comes to people ...' he let his voice drop, 'take care what you say, John. Wait now, I'm coming up. Don't say any more.' He looked up, putting his finger to his lips. He turned away.

As Logan turned a soft little bear hit the nape of his neck and fell at his feet. Thrown from above—but from which window? From his frightened child overhead, or the wailing one next door? Or from a spiteful mother, cunningly aiming so that he should never, never know? He looked round. The windows of both houses were empty, but though there was no movement and now no sound from either side, he knew he was being watched. He stooped and gingerly picked up the bear. It was slightly

10

damp, limp and dirty, and its cold pink eyes were specked with mud. Nevertheless it was still tenaciously holding to its part of teddy-bear. Logan was tempted to drop it, kick it away into some place where it could be later recovered and quietly got rid of. He had no wish to make a show of himself for the neighbours. His one idea was to do the job in private without fuss or words, for he was cold and tired and his encounter with the underworld of bears had worn him out for that night. But he knew this was not possible. Something more hung on it. There was a ritual to be observed, for behind him was someone absolutely intent on seeing what he would do.

Logan stepped out of the shadow of the house onto the grass. He was a large, heavy man and now he made himself taller. He stiffened himself, bracing his legs against the ground as though for a feat of strength. He raised the bear above his head in one hand, shaking it slightly, and at the same time called loudly over his shoulder to the open windows: 'The bear-game's over! Do you hear that—all of you? Finished! There'll be no more bear talk here! Watch this. Here's the end of it!' Along the silent row of houses one or two curtains were cautiously parting and somewhere a hammering ceased. A few wives and husbands were being beckoned to windows.

'Finished!' shouted Logan. He lowered his arm, ran forward over the grass and up the path again towards the wilderness beyond. Still running he swung his arm up and back over his head. He flung the bear as high and as far as he could towards the pond. There was a moment of silence, stretched so long that he thought of the bear hanging spreadeagled somewhere deep inside a tree. But suddenly he heard a rushing crackle of twigs and then a faint, far splash. He imagined he saw the black circles rippling

11

further and further out until at last there was only a gentle folding along the banks, and in the centre an absolute calm.

Logan turned. Casually he brushed his hands together, bent to dust off the knees of his trousers, and started to walk slowly back up the path towards his house. He felt his limbs relax as he opened the back door. The place was grey enough after the gloom of the garden. The living-room had the usual desolate air, carefully disguised by its few gimmicky coloured ornaments. The hall was chill as ever. But a palpable relief, like the glow from a hidden skylight, came directly down from above. And a sound which made him stare. At the top of the stairs his child stood laughing.

Wheels

Many a time the professor boasted of the work which he managed to get done in trains as he went from town to town, giving lectures to societies and papers to conferences. Even at his own post in the university he was continually on the move, for he lived a long way out of the city and thought nothing of making the daily journey, there and back, throughout the three terms. When his colleagues, sitting snugly wedged between desk and fireplace in book-lined studies, described their methods and times of work, he took a greater pleasure in describing his own. And in a community where new eccentricities were hard to come by, his was fairly easy to convey. He could frankly say that he had no regular place of work—or rather, no fixed place. A railway carriage, swaying and rattling through un-familiar fields and villages was, as often as not, his only study for weeks on end.

On long journeys he would spread papers along the seat and stack his books on the rack. When he had the carriage to himself, as he often had, he found that it helped him in working out some single, difficult problem, to move constantly from one window to the other across a space which took him only two short steps to cover. Here he was safely confined as in a cell, and he found it stimulating to be able to look from the one world where he worked into another which whirled past so close that he could almost touch the yellow weed on the banks or the sides of tunnels as they rattled through. Yet nothing could reach him from this world except the pollen or soot blown in on windy days, or the occasional dandelion seeds which settled between the pages of his books and floated out, blown by his vehement breath, days later in the lecture room. No sound from outside could reach him either. Sometimes he passed long rows of men with sledge-hammers striking on iron bars, close to the line, or children ran forward from nearby houses, shouting and trailing sticks and pieces of tin along the corrugated fences separating rail from gardens. But he could watch the swinging arms and open mouths, framed by the window, as he might watch a piece of extravagant miming. Even thunderstorms could break overhead to be recognized only by an unnatural flicker of light in the glass of some advertisement opposite, if he happened to raise his head in time.

The professor's feeling for trains was no passing phase or obsession left over from childhood. It had grown stronger as he had grown stronger in his own powers, and nowadays it was not so much a love of trains as an absolute identification with them. Many of the phrases he used to describe the thoughts and actions of human beings might have applied as well to the movement of wheels and pistons. He liked to feel that his own mind worked with the energy and control of a powerful engine—not simply mechanically propelled, but fed and illumined by fire itself. At the long halts in stations he would sometimes get off and walk up to the top of the train to watch the fuel being shovelled in—dull, lifeless nuggets changing miraculously into fire and speed. As far as he was concerned, most of the men he knew dealt in nuggets which remained grey nuggets—capable at best of keeping some domestic fire going for a few hours at a time. He knew it was not so with him.

He was a man in his middle fifties—tall and very thin. His large head, except for the half-cap of reddish hair, was round and bare—bare it seemed rather than bald, for there was nothing vulnerable or ageing about this head. He considered his brain to be his chief weapon, and the bareness of his head was like the bareness of a powerful bludgeon with which he was able to defend himself at all times. Although he was not known to take any particular form of exercise, he moved with deliberate ease and an economy of energy which suggested that he had solved not only some of the harder problems of language, but that he had himself under control and had solved the problem of well-regulated movement right down to the joints of his fingers. The only exaggerated movement he ever made was an occasional side-to-side swing of his head when he was particularly tired, as though, whatever else happened, he had to keep his head smoothly moving, constantly on the look-out for attack from any quarter. He had a long, curved problem-probing nose, a pugnacious chin outlined but not softened by a short beard, and he was fond of saying that it was his long experience in argument which had kept him young and active as any other fighter. He had never settled into a rut like so many people of his age, and he believed he owed much of his liveliness to the train journeys which he made all the year round.

The clichés of academic praise which sometimes appeared in reviews of his work or were spoken from college platforms in votes of thanks, though they occasionally irritated him, seemed to sum up something of what he felt about himself as he travelled from one railway station to another about the countryside. Such phrases as: '... the professor goes straight for his objective ... ruthless and unswerving ... without wasting any time on the way ... new horizons opening out on every side as he drives us before him with his accustomed energy ...' These, he felt, had more than a hint of truth. It was not that he didn't notice the life around him. In trains and out of them, people were surprised at how much he could relate of his journeys. He had an extraordinary facility for reading the names of unfamiliar stations from express trains. He could decipher posters and even newsbills while flying through at ninety miles an hour. But for him the real fascination lay in the fact that he could leave them all— places, people, and all the far-strewn junk of their habitations—far behind forever in only a few seconds. The professor was not given to dramatizing himself, but when the subject of death came up he had been heard to remark jokingly—but at the same time making wide, unexpected gestures of acceptance with his long arms—that he could not imagine himself sinking passively into oblivion in his bed or in an armchair. The most likely end for a man like himself would be a train-crash—his spirit whirling off like a still-glowing spark from a machine which, only a few minutes before, had been going full steam ahead into the darkness. At times like these he made it seem a matter of surprise and regret that he had not been born in a railway station.

The professor was not happy in the long summer vacation unless he was speeding from one place to another. It was not enough for him to take a pile of books and papers to the seaside, or to try and enjoy himself wandering about the continent as many of his colleagues did. He disliked the whole idea of holidays, especially as so many uninformed people imagined that his having a Chair meant that he could sit in it comfortably for at least five months of every year. He spent a good deal of time and nervous energy analysing, modifying and correcting this view wherever it showed itself. But as he was nearly always travelling to Summer Schools or conferences in the long vacation, he found his free time easier to describe than many other men in his position.

'What do I do with my free time?' He would take up the question with a smile which felt good-natured to the muscles of his own face, but made a disturbing impression on the person opposite. 'Well, there it is, if you want to call it *free* time,' he would go on, recklessly shuffling the pile of papers on his knee and producing from amongst them a programme of close-set dates, divided into hours and minutes and stretching on through all the summer months. After such an encounter many an innocent holiday-maker stepped off the train thinking himself lucky indeed to be getting his week's holiday at the seaside. But hardened travellers like the professor himself countered his move by producing mysterious lists of their own, engagement diaries black with names, and even maps on which they traced their devious routes around the country. Unless he was careful to whom he spoke, the professor often found himself engaged in this battle of wits over the question of who took the shortest holiday in the year. As often as not he scored his point simply by the abstracted gaze with which he listened to other people's information, and the impression he gave, at the same time, of struggling to concentrate on matters of infinitely greater importance.

One summer the professor was invited to give a course of lectures to a new group which, a year or so before, had taken over a small and unknown castle as their headquarters. It was not quite the usual Summer School, but run on informal conference lines by a group of high-principled students and teachers, for the benefit of undergraduates over a wide area. Nor were the undergraduates the usual ones to be found at summer gatherings. All of them had lately recovered from serious illness, physical or mental, and were preparing to take up their studies the following winter. The Castle Group, as it was called, had been formed to help them over this period of adjustment and to give them, over a few weeks, a mixture, both soothing and stimulating, of convalescent home and holiday camp, plus an injection of learning given by experts between ten and twelve-thirty in the morning. For healthy guests and convalescents, strong enough to hear the opinions of their fellows, there were special discussion groups in the late evening, centred about one guest speaker. Religion did not appear on the programme in black and white, but it pervaded the atmosphere like a bracing air in which it would seem a great ingratitude not to thrive and grow healthier in body and spirit day by day. Though up till now the place had been used only by British students of the most orthodox belief and behaviour, the Castle Group made a point of being wide open to all races, creeds and forms of worship. A minimum of religious terms was used when the leaders met together to discuss further means of widening the way in, and at all times God was awaited cheerfully and good-humouredly as might be the visits of a distinguished doctor or psychiatrist. The invitation which had gone out to the professor was a conscious token of their extraordinary tolerance rather than a recognition of his own special gifts.

The atmosphere of toleration was formidable. Though still a long way from his destination, the professor felt it the moment he stepped from the train and faced the three young men who had come to drive him the next ten miles to the castle. He could see at a glance they were not going to be the sharp-witted characters whom he welcomed above all others at such a gathering—people who could be counted on to send the blood to his head and force him to bring out the sharpest and subtlest arguments he had in store. Instead he saw, with a lowering of spirits, that they were determined to take him to their hearts on the spot. Their greeting was lost in the shriek of the train's whistle, but their smiles and the long, welcoming arms held out to him made up for any loss of words. Before the smoke had dissolved above the platform he was hurried out of the station with only time for him to give one last look at the train as it curved the bend.

With it, as far as he was concerned, went the source of his power, and the means of his escape. But by this time he was well used to the routine. For the next few days he would demonstrate his mind at work in a way which would make it plain that though most other brains were composed of spongy tissue—wheels of steel and vibrating wires had replaced this in his own. He would make a swift and powerful impression, and after the week a train would rescue him from their midst and renew him for the next encounter. Nevertheless, today as he was driven further and further into the country along a rough, winding road, he had a sense of foreboding. Although the gesture seemed discourteous to the young men, who had already begun to point out places of interest in the surrounding country, he felt impelled to pull out his timetable every now and then to make sure of the exact time of his returning train. Even this gesture was unnecessary. For many years back he had made it his business to know the whole timetable off by heart.

As a rule the professor enjoyed arriving at out-of-the-way places, but the first sight of this place was not reassuring. A broad forbearance seemed to have spread from the house to its surroundings, flattening and removing all obstacles so that the approach was as open and lacking in mystery as the drive up to a modern bungalow. Students, digging for the health of body and spirit, had levelled small hills and cut down great trees. Where it had been impossible to heave up boulders embedded in the roots of old trees, rock gardens had been planted and half a dozen home-made garden seats, rigidly constructed for meditation rather than romance, had been wedged into unscreened corners. Behind the building the rough ground was marked with rows of tattered vegetables, and in the square patch of earth, newly cut from the moorland and destined to be an orchard, a few frail seedling trees had survived their first winter's blasts. In the first few minutes on arrival inside the castle itself visitors felt they had been cheated by the name of the place. It looked, at first glance, no more than a hundred years old, and obviously owed its name simply to the castellated outline of its roof and the turrets at either end, smooth as ornamental biscuit tins. But old or new, no atmosphere could in any case have survived in the bracing air created by relays of enthusiastic men and women who'd come together to demonstrate that with co-operation and toleration, a home could be made out of a Victorian castle and a garden out of a wilderness. There were limits to what could be done however, and the roads which led eastwards down towards the coast and up into the hills on the other side were as rough as any in that part of the country. It seemed to the professor, as he looked about the place, that there were no cars on the road except for the ramshackle one in which he had arrived. Instead, he observed with a sinking heart that most able-bodied people, amongst both staff and students, were going about on bicycles.

The professor had paid very little attention to bicycles since he was a boy. For him they lacked all power and fire, and were scarcely to be thought of as machines at all. But now, a handsome bike being lent to him on arrival, he had to think about them, examine them and talk about them for a good part of each day. He discovered it was not enough to lecture in the mornings and galvanize the fireside discussions in the evening. The younger men were also expected to accompany one or other of the picnic-study groups which set off on bicycles every afternoon into the surrounding countryside. The professor had never doubted that he belonged, at least in spirit, to the younger group. The weather was fine, the young men and women eager and stronger than he had ever expected convalescents to be, and they had a healthy outlook on learning which led them to choose high sites with panoramic views for their study places. More than once during the first days of his visit it occurred to the professor that it was not so difficult to account for the unclaimed bike he'd been given. Some genuine, unsuspecting convalescent had probably succumbed under the strain of his first days at the castle, dying without fuss and leaving his brand-new bike as a gift to the community. From the size and weight of the thing, he thought it was more than likely to outlive its owner by many, many years.

Very often the professor was not able to speak when he arrived on the heights. His silences, though still impressive, became longer after each outing. Even when he'd recovered his breath it was a new experience for him to have to hurl his words, not into the respectful hollow of a large class-room, but up into the open air, humming and whistling with a life of its own. The angry arguments with himself which were characteristic of his teaching, bursting back from four bare walls with a startling effect upon those who sat around, were now liable to be dispersed by chance currents of air. The few well-chosen words of criticism with which, indoors, he could quietly splinter someone's too-lengthy conclusion, so that this particular voice might not be heard again for hours or even days—these, out of doors, were as often as not interrupted by the honking of some unidentified bird in a nearby pond. He would then be lucky if there were not two or three bird-watchers amongst the group who would immediately get to their feet to investigate. For half the fun of these study-picnics—as had been so often pointed out to newcomers—was their spontaneity and informality. But above all it was the bicycle which prevented him from establishing an adequate image. After a few days the idea of himself as a highly-organized and streamlined machine for the destruction of nonsense had given way before an entirely new image which, little by little, was beginning to take its place.

It was difficult to avoid seeing it. Wherever he looked, in front or behind, he saw arched, bony spines and eager necks craning forward over handlebars, and legs which pedalled furiously or laboriously on, mile after mile. But when he looked at himself he was aware simply of a pair of extraordinarily shaped knees which moved up and down under his eyes—not with the regularity of well-oiled pistons —but with the cracking, straining, knobbled movement of ill-fitting joints of wood. He was fascinated by these knees as he had now time to study them in the greatest detail, even to the slow shredding of threads at the trouser-knees as the cloth stretched to ripping point and abruptly slackened. He watched these knees bulging grotesquely to take a steep road, and unknotting and softening on a straight one. He saw them fixed and bent motionless on a downward slope, the trouser-knees ballooning into a fat shape in the breeze. He seldom took his eyes off them to look around and never spoke until he had reached his destination, when he would put his feet to the ground with unnatural caution like a man treading suspected bogland.

In spite of the successful morning and evening sessions the professor found that the afternoons occupied much of his concentration and energy. The tremendous driving power which sustained him until lunchtime and which, up till now, had broken down defences and opened up endless vistas of self-doubt for his students, began to be seriously sapped by the cycle runs and picnic teas. It now took him all his time to work up sufficient speed and power for the evening attack. A half-hearted discussion on 'Conscience versus Chaos' or 'Psychoanalysis in the Moral Framework' could go on for some time around him before he could bring himself to destroy it. His silence, which could once have been interpreted as a gathering together of his forces, was now caused simply by a limpness in his limbs and a lightness in his head due to the morning's efforts.

But he was biding his time. Only another two days, and they would be accompanying him back to the station. He saw it all with an exhilarating clearness—how he would stare down as they pedalled like mad along the road beside the railway line, vainly trying to keep up with the train as it gathered speed until at last they fell far behind, a collection of shiny, round-backed creatures creeping after him in

23

the distance. He would never again set hands on a bicycle for as long as he lived.

The evening before he was due to leave the Warden of the Castle Group waylaid the professor as he was coming out of his final after-supper discussion group. On the whole it had been a successful evening. He had mustered together all his remaining powers for a last effort, so that there should be no question of remembering him by a bent back and jerking knees, but by a cannonade of questions and answers plus a final series of hammer-blows, aimed at putting a bent argument back into shape. An excess of emotion had crept into an argument on good and evil. He had had to raise his voice above it all, calling out in anguished tones:

'I don't think I quite understand what is being said here —perhaps I am being particularly stupid this evening. But if you could repeat your argument again very, very slowly this time, defining the terms you are using—simply for my benefit—then quite possibly we can begin to communicate with one another again!'

But in five minutes the session was over, and the professor left in triumph without getting back into communication with anyone. He scarcely felt the plucking at his sleeve as he went down the corridor to his room, yet he realized at once, by the expression on the man's face when he got inside the door, that the Warden was going to appeal to the best in him. He was accustomed to that look. In the past he had known how to counter it. But this time his heart misgave him. The man had already gone a long way with his proposition before he could brace himself to interrupt.

'... I hardly know how we can ask you to do this,' the man was saying, '... but if you could possibly give us a

24

few more days of your time. There was already a big gap in the programme owing to Professor Haddow's sudden illness. And now this morning we hear that Dr Pollock has been held up indefinitely at a conference on the Continent. Indeed he doubts whether he'll be with us for another ten days at least ... both men of outstanding gifts, as you yourself know. But in present circumstances, if I may say so, you happen to be the only man who, in my opinion, could quite easily stand in place of both of them put together.' The Warden lowered his voice discreetly at this point and glanced round as if the two men might have unexpectedly returned together and be standing close behind him to do him some injury. Then he turned to the professor again, opening the palms of his hands in appeal.

At any other time the professor could have summoned up a dozen suitable excuses for getting away. But the moment for a swift and final refusal went by. As the other man murmured further compliments and pleas for help, he experienced a new sensation which he diagnosed as a morbid softening in the region of his heart and a renewed limpness in his limbs, not unlike what he experienced after a day's cycling. For a moment, as he let himself in for another week at the Castle, he felt scarcely able to stand on his two legs and, as soon as he was alone, sank, exhausted, into an armchair.

The following afternoon, from the high slopes of a hill overlooking the country, the professor caught a glimpse of the train which should have taken him away from the place forever. He heard it rattling down through the valley below and saw its windows reflecting the evening sun in a series of challenging flashes. But he could no longer identify with it. It was the first time in years he had failed to be at the station for the time he'd planned, and seven long and exhausting days would go by before he caught the next train. He vowed, as his eyes followed its windings, that he was not going to be made a fool of on two wheels in the meantime. Under his hands the bicycle could be revolutionized. In a very short time, if he put everything he'd got into the job, he could turn it into a genuine machine, worthy of the name. Had he not supplied abundant sparks and engine power to situations far more difficult than this? From that moment he began to discipline himself for the task ahead.

It was easy enough, he discovered, when whizzing downhill in front of the rest of them, to straighten his back, stiffen his knees, and generally smooth himself into what he considered to be a streamlined shape. He could even manage to throw out a few words to those coming on behind and foresaw the time when it might be possible to carry on a vivid discussion with anyone who could keep up with him. The countryside did not interest him, but he was even able to look about him now and then with the keen glances of the nature-lover. It was only on the following day that he began to see he'd set himself a major task. The cycling group, working on the rule that it was better to aim at several goals in an afternoon rather than one, had planned an expedition combining the usual picnic-study with a visit to a stone circle which stood five or six miles east of the castle and on the highest point of the moor.

It was not a difficult climb, but it was a steady one. The professor laid hold of his machine like a racing-cyclist. He set himself to concentrate on the road ahead as he had never done before. But at best he could manage little more than a walking speed, and he scarcely felt the movement of the wheels beneath him. What he did have was a close-up view of every detail of the ground for miles on end, and as he stared down, his eyes bulging with effort, his mouth open, he looked like a naturalist continually amazed at the pebbles and earth, feathers, twigs and insects slowly passing beneath his eyes. But the professor was not at all amazed. He disliked the slow-motion close-up, and to him one pebble was so much like another that it was as if he'd been staring at the same patch of road all afternoon. He was grateful for even the smallest change in the colour of the earth, or of the extra skill involved in manoeuvring a particularly stony part of the road. But there was little choice. In the end he was simply glad that by staring beyond the front wheel he could keep his eyes off his knees which appeared more grotesque the longer he looked at them. Yet in spite of it all, he managed to look an impressive figure as he bent over the handlebars. Somehow he had begun to infuse his bike with his own importance. It no longer looked the wobbling, uncontrolled vehicle it had been when he first laid hands on it. It was now a machine, steely and efficient, and it made a rut behind him on the road deep and straight as a motorbike's.

Nevertheless, while the convalescents grew stronger every day the professor grew more exhausted. Sometimes a series of minute, red wheels would spin before his eyes as he bent to put on his shoes in the morning, and his dreams were disturbed by the never-ending whirring of bicycle tyres floating miraculously over the deep sand of deserts or skimming the grass of lush meadows. Time and again he slept through his alarm which had begun to sound in his dreaming ears more and more like the urgent ringing of hundreds of bicycle bells. Younger men on the staff, who had long ago given up all forms of exercise, began to come up and congratulate him—not on his agility in discussion, his unfailing grip of fundamentals, but on his endurance on the machine, his enviable speed and balance.

Meantime he did his best to keep up his own work, and whenever he had a couple of hours to himself he took up the learned article he was writing. It was usual for him to go at it with great force and verve. These last days however the energy had been missing. Laboriously he wound out the words—words without spark or speed. Ideas which a few weeks ago would have fired him now lay smoothly, with a deadly flatness, on the page. The thing was in slow-motion, and once or twice during the last days there had come to mind that one word which he could not hear without a shudder of nervous laughter when it was applied to other men's work—the word 'pedestrian'. But it was not walking which had brought him to this pass. His mind was working with the smooth, mechanical action of a pair of bicycle wheels softly whirring along a dead level road.

There was no longer any need for the professor to show himself master of anything. All his movements by this time had become mechanized. He was free to concentrate his attention on one thing, and one thing only. He began to resemble one of those pale-faced racing cyclists with furrowed brows and bitten lips who look neither to right nor left but grimly in front to some distant goal. He lived simply from day to day, from hour to hour, and the goal before him, now almost in sight, was the welcoming plume of smoke he would see as he neared the station—the smoke from a train which was oiled, stoked and breathing out fire for his deliverance.

The good weather held to the last. The professor was able to refer to this at the farewell lunch party given in his honour on the day he was due to leave. 'It has enabled me to do more—much more than I had ever thought was

28

possible in the time,' he said, leaning heavily on the table and looking across with jaundiced eyes at the row of enthusiastic faces which stared up at him. 'It has enabled me to see endless places of interest which I should otherwise never have known—to see castles, forts, ancient bridges and prehistoric monuments. I have seen the countryside,' he added as a bitter afterthought. For a second he allowed himself to glance behind him through the windows where, for the first time in two weeks, the heavy thunderclouds were blowing up for rain. 'I might otherwise have seen almost nothing,' he went on after a long pause. The first drops of rain streaked the glass. Even now he automatically looked about him for the convalescents, for even one to whom he could address himself. But these faces seemed rounder and rosier, their eyes brighter than ever. He searched conscientiously, however, until he found a young man sitting at the opposite end of the table who, even from a distance, seemed to show distinct signs of ill-health. There was something rigid and ill-at-ease about the fellow. Under the professor's gaze he held his head stiffly bent, now and then stroking his brow with nervous fingers.

'But best of all,' the professor went on, still staring at the withdrawn face at the end of the table, 'it has enabled me to get to know some of you young people—particularly those less fortunate in health—and to share in this experience, to become for a short time one of yourselves—if you will allow me to put it like that ...'

At this point the man, who had been shifting uneasily under the morbidly sympathetic gaze of the professor, looked up with an expression of undisguised annoyance and dislike. The professor hastily removed his eyes. This was no undergraduate. He recognized at once the newly-appointed lecturer at his own college—a man nearly his

29

own age who now showed, as he raised his head, a heavy jowl whose hard-living crimson was slowly beginning to suffuse his face. The professor ventured no further remarks. After the lunch was over he spent a quiet hour getting his things together, while running through the timetable again to verify his train and to examine various other unlikely and complicated rail connections throughout the British Isles.

He was summoned earlier than he expected by one of the young men who had driven him from the station a fortnight ago. Already on the main drive a crowd had gathered to see him off. He was not suprised to see them there. He had worked hard and he had worked overtime. He had made his mark on them but he did not intend them to see that they had made their mark on him. He didn't smile as he made his way through the midst of them, for it was not his habit to respond to a large number of smiling faces. He bowed and nodded, waiting for a clear way to be made for him to reach the waiting car. Although used to all kinds of student antics he was not ready for the way in which, at a command, they fell out into two long lines, making a sort of bridal passage for him to walk up; and he was taken aback to see that three young men, smiling more broadly than the rest, awaited him at the top of the line. It was the man in the middle who displeased him most. He was holding onto a bicycle, familiar to the professor in every dent and scar. But as he drew nearer he saw that, overnight, it had been transformed. Not a speck of mud or rust could be seen. Here and there the enamel had been touched up, the leather of the saddle shone, and the wheels had been scraped and polished until they glittered like a new machine. On the handle-bars were tied two colourful labels which the professor could not at once bring himself to read. But there was no need to. A silence fell as the young man started his speech. It was a better speech than the professor had given at lunch. It was more simple and spontaneous, and the boy's voice rang with deep, genuine feeling.

'It has come as a surprise to us all,' he said, still gripping the handlebars with white-knuckled enthusiasm, 'to find that the professor who has shown himself such a fanatical cyclist, has actually got no cycle of his own. That's an odd thing, isn't it? You might call it eccentricity—for a man to forgo the very thing that brings him keenest pleasure. Some day perhaps he'll be able to explain this himself— if we're lucky enough to have him again as lecturer. All the same, he mustn't suppose that this is in the nature of a presentation. How could it be? As he knows himself, it's not even a new bike. But it *is* a good one—one of the very best on the market today. I think our distinguished guest can vouch for that!' His eyes met the professor's for an instant, and after a pause he went on in a rather lower voice: 'If our funds had been in better shape, nothing would have given us more pleasure than to present him, here and now, with an absolutely up-to-the-minute model. As it is, we've made this almost like new again. We must simply ask him if he will accept it as an inadequate but genuine expression of our gratitude for the extra time he's spent here, and for all the energy he's put out on our behalf. We would like to feel that he'll come back, and very soon, on another longer visit. Meantime—happy cycling!'

The professor was not aware of answering, any more than a man in a dream is aware of replying to the thundering voices of fate. But from the burst of applause he gathered that he'd spoken some words before climbing into the car. The return journey to the station was exactly as he had expected it to be, but for certain details which had been beyond his imagination at the time. He was escorted for some distance along the way by a drove of eager cyclists, but well in front of them all rode the smiling young man on a machine which had the professor's name written in large, block capitals on the labels. The car went very slowly on the rough roads towards the station, but the cyclists soon fell behind. Now and then his driver winced sideways from the belligerent arm which the professor thrust out in order to consult his watch, but some little time went past before he noticed that both the fists of his passenger were clenched, and that certain veins had lived up to their classic description of 'standing out' on the professor's forehead.

'I wonder if you are aware how much it matters to me that I should catch this train?' the menacing voice said close to his ear after they had driven a mile or two in silence, interrupted by a few faltering pleasantries from the young man. The professor was now leaning so near that he found some difficulty in lifting his elbows to the steering wheel.

'It is a matter of the greatest urgency,' the professor went on, pressing his sharp knees dangerously in amongst the brakes.

'If I don't get off on this train, I must ask to be driven the ninety miles to my destination. There will be no question of my waiting for a later train. It would be better for you, I think, if you accelerate now, and if you would keep absolutely silent while doing so.'

There were no further words between them. The young man sat low in his seat and his neck was as rigid as a racing-motorist on the last mile of the track. Each time the car bounced his face grew pale, and on the roughest stretches it grew contorted as though he carried a load of high explosive on the seat beside him.

They arrived early for the train and the professor had been in his seat a good fifteen minutes before the cyclists came panting up alongside. There was just time for his bike to be taken to the luggage van, and he watched from the corridor as with reassuring nods in his direction, they lifted it gently in—then lined up at the edge of the platform to wave goodbye as the train drew out. He noticed that the young man who had driven him was not waving. There was a thoughtful expression on his face, as though only lately had he looked down into the darker places of the human spirit. The rest made a dash for their bicycles as the train drew out and the last glimpse he had of them was the flash of wheel after wheel as they started pedalling furiously back the way they had come.

The professor was alone in his carriage. For a long time he sat quite still, staring before him and trying to gather together strength as the train gathered speed. And like a patient intent on therapeutic treatment, he concentrated simply on the vibrations which travelled up from the soles of his feet and down the length of his spine where, even through the plushy back of the seat, he could feel the powerful drag of the engine now going full steam ahead. Still he sat on, only opening his eyes occasionally to stare sideways out at the smoke coiling past his window, stained green in the afternoon light. Above him on the luggage rack his bulging briefcase bounced gently on top of his suitcase. Everything was again in rhythmical motion. He had only to lean back to be regenerated. Simply by laying his hand along the hot, vibrating seat he would be revived.

But something stood in the way of recovery; and though

his mind, trained rigorously over the years to reject the superfluous, made a tremendous effort to dispel it, he was unsuccessful. For it was not only contained in his head. He knew that at the far end of the train, moving to the rhythm of the heavy wheels which carried him swiftly away from unpleasant memories, another pair of wheels, bearing his name, bounded lightly but triumphantly along with him.

Out of Hand

These nightly wrestlings with newspaper began quietly.
A faint rustling of pages—giving no more warning of
turmoil than the first, surreptitious scrapes of leaves in
the night. After all, they were less than the familiar
cracklings with which, throughout the years and yards of
newsprint, the old man had displayed his massive dis-
content with the world. Hadn't he all his life ravaged and
worried the pages the better to get to grips with the clots
of black headline which hid in the folds before he'd got
the paper properly opened up? With one brisk shake and
a bounce-up of his bony knee, he would free the poisonous
black cockroach of print from its crack, revealing it in all
its rustling insect slyness. It was a poisonous world but he'd
kept up with it, following it step by step on its downward
path. Yes, it was going down. No, it had not been better
in his young days nor in his father's either! He did not fall
into that particular trap laid for him by his clever middle-
aged children and his clever teenage grandchildren, nor
even by the clever, impudent newsboy who hurled the
paper in at the open window in summertime or used it as
a brush to whiffle off balls of snow from the hedge in
winter. No, and no better in his grandfather's either!
There was no first or last place on a downward slope, no one
part worse than another on the sheer curve that had

35

started as soon as human beings had anything to do with it. All this—explosive cracklings, exclaimings and paper-jabbings—had been a natural part of every day. But this year his verbal protests had grown less. During one week he made only two remarks as he sat with his paper on his lap. When words stopped the rustlings increased prodigiously. And they were of an unfamiliar kind.

He would lift the paper high in the air and lay it down again slowly and with infinite care on his knee, softly smoothing out the flaws with the back of his hands, would stare at it for a while, pick it up, fold it back from the centre, lay it down again and begin painstakingly creasing down a long thin edge with his thumb, lift it up, open it out and fold it back, lay it down again and softly pleat its edge, take it up, shake it out and stare at it for a long time. Sometimes he would give the whole thing an almighty shake-up, pages would drop out and he would lift them from the floor, contemptuous, on the toe of his shoe, and fit them together again with a flailing of his angry arms around his head. He sat now in a continual whirlwind of moving paper.

'He hasn't read a word for weeks. You know that, of course,' said his grand-daughter one night after he had gone to bed. It was a windy autumn night and the gusts blew everything towards the window. They heard the leaves, dust, the hard pellets of rain—and other less familiar sounds—twigs or the dry snappings of insects jet-propelled against glass, siftings and slidings and the brush of the bending tree on the wall. No one spoke. After a few minutes the girl looked round again at her father, her mother and her brother, and answered herself briskly: 'That's right. I've been watching him. He's folding up.' Her mother, daughter of the old man, looked taken aback

36

not so much at this phrase as at the briskness with which it was uttered. Though she was a quick and opinionated woman herself, she became very slow, very vague, when the word 'death' came up. She thought a lot about it though, and from time to time she moved about the idea of her own death as though padding softly in bedroom slippers round an invalid's bed. The man's approach was different. On most things his opinions were cautious, but on the subject of death he could be boisterous. If ever the word was thrown out in company, he made a grab at it, bounced it about like a hard ball from hand to hand, giving it a kick now and then to send it up. He could be kinder than his wife, but about people's deaths—the sudden over-forties anyway—he was sorry, cheerful and rather ruthless, his view being that there was not much you could say about death and about a possible after-life—nothing at all. He talked a lot all the same. And it was he who now answered his daughter:

'Folding up, is he? Why, isn't he well? I'd even say he was a lot better, physically, than last year.'

She insisted. 'Folding himself up is nearer it. I've watched him all this week and that's exactly how it looks.' There was some discussion about colour and appetite and the doctor's opinion. The girl was stubborn and after a time they all fell silent and went on with what they'd been doing. The woman was knitting something for herself in bright orange wool on huge needles. It was going to take days not months, and she was using an up-to-the-minute pattern. All the same she now knitted very rapidly indeed, as though to dispel some distant or not so distant image of herself. Her husband went back to his own paper. He turned the pages, when he had to, briskly and neatly, taking care to make as little noise and fuss about it as possible.

Much later the girl went to make coffee for herself and her brother followed, catching up the old man's newspaper from the rug on the way out. 'What exactly are you trying to say about him?' he asked when they were on their own in the kitchen.

'Every time I open my mouth you ask what I'm trying to say. It's become a habit. And a bad one.'

'No, I'm interested.'

'I'm not trying. This is what I mean. I do think he's wrapping it up. Would it be strange at that age?'

'Not at all. But what interests me is what goes on behind it all. Who or what is he wrapping?'

'Sometimes he's tucking himself in. Sometimes smoothing himself out. Once in a while he flings it all up and kicks himself free again.'

'A do-it-yourself dying?'

'Well, if ever a thing's to be done alone, this is it.'

'To my mind it's a tidying up. The nearest thing to it is that park attendant across there, coming in after the week-end. No sooner in the gate but he's tying up and wrapping and jabbing and sometimes kicking. I wouldn't get in his way for worlds. A mixture of fury and for-bearance. Do you mind talking about the old man?'

'No, I mind for him though. I hope he manages to his satisfaction. He's had some grudges in his day.'

'So it's the world he's tidying up.'

'If it is he's got his work cut out. He's been a regular angry old man for years.'

They were silent. The boy lifted up a corner of the paper and held it, ducking his head sideways to look. It had been a rough week—so bad it had been difficult to fit the dark stuff into the columns apportioned for it. Natural catastrophe and human violence jostled for precedence.

Chunks of distant stuff had to be cut drastically for injuries nearer home. Famine had made shift for riot and yesterday's hurricane was already howled down by angry mobs in Europe. The boy glanced over all this, but he also examined closely the actual stuff of the paper. For there were two kinds of reading here. As well as the print there were the pleats that his grandfather had made, the crumples he had attempted to smooth. To the boy this also seemed important.

'All the same, he's going to take his time about it,' he said at last, putting down the paper as though having made a careful diagnosis of its skin creases. 'I hope to God we'll manage it.'

'How *we'll* manage?'

'Certainly. Look how the evening's folded up already. Everyone stuck in his own thoughts. Silent.'

'But how about us? Don't we talk?'

'A bit. There's still chunks of stuff we don't even touch. I don't feel I'm saying the half.'

As a family they got on well. Outside, in their official family roles of parent, grandparent, son and daughter, they had all of them thrown themselves dutifully into the divided generations debate, the endless age-group wrangle. But with forced gusto. The heart wasn't exactly in it. They liked one another. Yet at the same time it was true that this idea of death—even an old man's death—had divided them a bit. In the end—and barring the catastrophe which hung over everyone—it could be boiled down to a practical matter of year-counting. And the family counts came out different. The old man was beyond it, his grandchildren hadn't begun, and the father and mother, consciously or not, were counting all the time— counting out the years of their life as though, at some

39

unspecified mid-term, a time-watch had been placed at their elbow, silent, but working industriously away. At any moment the alarm could buzz. How many of their friends had lately been staggered by such alarms—struck down by heart attacks or suicidal depressions, slowly or shatteringly waking up to cancer, to coronaries, finding the harmless stiffness in the finger dangerously related to the stiffness in the toe, the familiar headache turned menacing, the cough which had kept them company for years turned killing? Even pleasures could now be counted with a sense of loss. The once-a-year friends, the once-in-two-years' travels. Sometimes the questions burst with appalling force. How many more times would they actually see this person, visit that country? Twenty for some things, ten for others. Five, three or less. None perhaps if you happened to be too ambitious. Was the Far East finally out then? Greenland's mountains still in the question-mark bracket? The old desire for South America came back in force, stripped of all sophisticated explanations about culture. Now it was raw, black longing. It was nothing more or less than the need to put an oar down into the thick mud of the Amazon river, to part the great glittering leaf-fronds overhead. You could say they actually hungered for crocodile. But not for the same crocodile. The idea that anyone should think them a contented couple with identical tastes seemed to drive them wild.

The fact that the old man had reached his eighty-second year was neither here nor there. It merely reminded them of their restlessness. There was nothing calm about him either, nothing resigned. He still struggled to get on top of the wilful paper, while rejecting utterly the soothing note that had crept into visitors' voices. But didn't people need comfort when they came to the end of their lives? What exactly did they need? Did this old unbeliever want re-assurance of some other existence?

'You never know what's going on in people's heads when they fall silent,' said the woman. 'They can change. They can change absolutely.' She was thinking about herself too. Her claim on a completely different kind of life. Here and now. When she said this her husband removed himself, but her son showed interest.

'You may want it,' he said. 'But does that make it any more likely?'

'Well at least I know the places are there. There are maps and photos. I could make the effort.'

'Which is different from a possible other existence. It can't be comprehended. So what efforts can you make towards it? Far less help anyone else. My guess is as good as yours—yours or an Archbishop's or a Himalayan hermit's.'

'People like us are always rushing in to shout that they're as well up, any day, as Archbishop, Pope or hermit.'

'And so they should. They've got to go on and on insisting that on certain things we're absolute ignoramuses, one and all. You can't let up for an instant!' But other uncalled-for questions on time cropped up in the midst of it all, and once in a while the woman could meditate by herself on the problem of when exactly a stole became a shawl with much the same solemnity as theologians discuss at what instant the body can be said to possess a soul.

Weeks later the independent old man entered a new stage in relation to his newspaper. Sometimes he would hand it over, open and scarcely crumpled, to whoever happened to be near with the brusque command: 'Here!' He waited, and as he waited he would fix that person with his eyes. It happened more often with neighbours who had

41

looked in, and they responded in various ways. Some took the paper and let it lie on their knees while they ran over it quickly to see if they could find the particular paragraph which demanded comment. And they would find some bit which they read out hesitatingly or pounced on, with an exclamation. No, they'd failed to hit the mark. The paper was at once withdrawn. Worst of all, when a woman neighbour, with unflinching, stubborn rectitude, insisted on reading aloud to him, working haphazardly down through robberies and recipes, crashes, rockets, round-table conferences and farmhouse murders—enunciating all benignly as a bedtime story—one with a sick twist here and there, but a bedtime story all the same. For a time the old man sat paralysed. Then in mid-sentence he left the room. They saw him pass the window outside, gesticulating, cautioning the disorderly clouds overhead and kicking up some dark, imagined dust from the paving-stones of the path. There were some who took the paper he offered, folded it and put it aside. Or used it to swat wasps. Or as a baton to conduct a conversation, as a fire-screen, as a lap-tray for a cup of tea. He watched angrily, incredulously or with desperate intensity as though at any moment they might hit on the one thing which would satisfy him. No one knew what he wanted. Did he know himself?

'He wants to be finished,' said the grand-daughter. 'And it all goes on. He goes on. The papers go on, the talk, the laughing, the coughing, the silence, plates coming and going, the forks and knives, dressing and undressing—day in day out, it all goes on. He's kept up with the world. Now there's the moon. The planets are coming into view. But the clouds are in the way, crumbs, dust—and paper, scraps of crumpled paper and falling pages. It's all got out of hand!'

Late one night, out of his hand, he let the paper slide to the floor. They heard the slow, rustling breath of the pages and above it the quick, rustling breath of the old man. It was a racer's breath, changing quickly from rustling to raucous as he put on the spurt towards his goal. The rims of his nostrils were hard and white as he sucked in the air. While the woman went to the phone his grandson crouched beside him and for a moment or two suffocated with him. But as suddenly the boy withdrew and his breath calmed. The gap between living and dying widened slowly, minute by minute. And soon the boy was no more than a sympathetic onlooker—glad to live and cool again like someone who has been ordered to step back and get on with his own business. He waited. There was now some division in his grandfather. While the upper part of his body still laboured for air, one hand felt along the ground at his side. He found the paper, handed it to the boy, at the same time turning his eyes to give him a look.

'All right. All right!' the boy said briskly. For a moment he knelt above the open pages wondering what he would do. The look had not been angry, nor appealing. It was wildly expectant. He began to fold the newspaper rapidly, turning it first one way then the other, creasing with his thumb and pressing down with his fist as he went. His own antics gave him the notion that this was a parcel he was making up. But it was parcelling done at speed as though a violent turmoil had to be smoothed and sealed, smoothed and sealed again and again until the frenzy of paper turned to a firm square and the square to a tight packet, hard as a little spade. Then the boy got up and started to fit it into the big, loose pocket of his grandfather's dressing-gown. It was a tough job but he managed to push the whole thing tightly down until the woollen flap covered it.

43

If only for this instant—chaos was contained. He stood back, silently congratulating himself and the old man on this prodigious feat. And immediately he saw the old man's hand come up and give the pocket a light, sharp tap. The strained head turned his way to signal its ironic, still undeceived, but unmistakable relief.

The Snow Heart

Following the first heavy snowfall of the year, a huge heart appeared on the bowling-green next to the hospital grounds. It was deeply marked out in the snow, and for sheer size—as seen from the height of the new hospital buildings—it was an eye-opener. It was the biggest shape that could be put inside the green without running over onto the surrounding paths; and whoever made it had been careful not to spoil his line. He had walked narrowly backwards, foot behind foot, and let his stick swallow up most of his prints. There was a line of chunky footsteps leading up to it, a line leading away, and no other marks.

The bowling-green was not connected with the hospital. High hedges made it private. Yet it was visible only from the hospital windows. All during summer and up till late autumn, when the green was closed, old men bent and swung their arms over a lawn smooth as a billiard table. Patients and visitors to the hospital were used to the sight of an endless turnover of players. There were bowlers strong as bulls down there as well as old men on their last legs. There were bossy bowlers and browbeaten bowlers. But whatever they were, domineering or defeated, the place was geared to age. Overnight the snow and the heart had changed all that. While the old men had been sleeping or sitting in their clubs or pubs their place had been smoothed out and engraved. A rejuvenation had taken place, and they were to know nothing of it.

The hospital staff were too busy in the morning to do much more than glance at the bowling-green in passing. It was left to the afternoon visitors who were always in the high corridor on Mondays, Wednesdays, Thursdays and at week-ends, waiting to be beckoned into certain medical and surgical wards on the stroke of three. The place where they waited was at the top of the building—a wide corridor with a staircase and a line of lifts at one end. Opposite were the swing doors leading through to the wards. On the window side it was almost entirely glass divided up by strips of metal and it was here that visitors lined up while they waited. They varied from day to day but most of them were long-distance people who had arrived early. Amongst these were the few who came to visit long-term patients and who formed a small in-group amongst the random coming and going of the rest. They were a clique who had their own private and sometimes silent language. They recognized one another and formed bonds even though they might have no clue to the other end of the attachment—the man, woman or child in the beds beyond.

On this particular afternoon half a dozen or so were waiting at the windows. They were glad, in a businesslike way, to see the snow. They were glad to see the heart. Any new thing at all on the way to the wards was something to be grateful for and visitors to long-term patients had to be particularly skilled collectors of news items, no matter how small or unimportant. Delivery of news was always a chancy affair. There was no knowing how long their patients might take over the bits they were given. Events which should have provided talk for an hour could be brushed aside in a matter of seconds. Patients had been known to listen

46

lackadaisically to news packets containing a cease-fire and a new war, and grasp at the tale of a bad egg in a bowl. To-day the early visitors at the window were too tired to go overboard for this heart. They had seen better last minute talking-points in their time. All the same they took it and filed it amongst other items where, with luck, it might fill a gap. While most of them collected it silently and turned to other things, one man remarked to the woman beside him that he would be telling his son about this.

'He'll be amused when I tell him,' he said. 'I mean the grotesque size of that thing will intrigue him.' It was a grave mistake indeed to make any pronouncement on what would or would not amuse or please one's patient. Few experienced visitors risked it. But there was a desperate streak in this man. The woman listened pleasantly to him and said that no doubt she too would be telling her daughter. But she knew it was a very different matter. The man's son had been here a long time and he would not get better. Her daughter, in a surgical ward, was getting better every day. Occasionally the man talked about his son, though rarely about his illness.

'He is rather difficult to please,' he had said one after-noon a few weeks earlier. 'He's inclined to find fault.' And some time after he had said: 'You know, he is very, very difficult to please. He finds fault with everything and everyone.'

'Poor fellow,' she had replied.

'And I'm afraid I irritate him,' said the father.

'Maybe,' she said. 'But of course it's not really you.'

'I don't know whether it's really me or not me. I just know I seem to irritate him more and more every day.'

One way or another the woman had got to know a bit about this man. His wife was dead, and there were not many other people to share the visits with him. His son, who had just finished his architect's training, had one good friend who wrote regularly from his new job in Canada. A few other friends took turns to visit him. Some had stopped for good. He'd had a girl friend once but she had disappeared early in his illness. 'Naturally enough—or unnaturally, whichever way you want to look at it,' said the man. There was this difficulty about hospitals and long-term visitors felt it most. As they went on it grew harder and harder to figure out what was natural and what was unnatural about the set-up. And it was not only the place which set them problems. They worried about themselves. Were they becoming less human or more human? And which was best under the circumstances? They sank and surfaced again, alternating in mood with those in the wards who sank and surfaced continually. The boy's father had been depressed himself for some time. But this afternoon he seemed cheerful, as though the snow, by levelling cracks and ridges and smoothing all anomalies of building and landscape, had made it possible to start again from the beginning.

The bowling-green was not the only thing visitors could look down at. The hospital was built round three sides of a large courtyard, and down there was a new fountain with two fish mouths which would one day blow water. There were a few newly-planted saplings, and three small flower beds sunk in the paving-stones, ready for planting. Triangles and oblongs of red, blue and yellow enamel had been set in a pattern along the side of the concrete wall which ran under the hedge on the bowling-green side. But the visitors, like ungrateful children, never looked at these things—or if they did it was only momentarily before staring above and beyond at scenes not intended for them.

48

They looked across at the windows of the west-wing wards. There they could see distant figures in beds—spry figures sitting bolt upright, half-reclining figures with knees sharply angled under red and blue blankets, and flat-out figures. The corridor people never wearied of this spectacle. It seemed that the people in the distant beds were more interesting and more mysterious than their own relatives in the nearby wards. This afternoon they looked across and saw the scene transformed. Bits of the outside world had invaded the inside. Nurses were moving about over there with caps white as the snowcaps on the chimney-pots. They were bouncing up pillows which were smaller versions of the fat snow-pillows below. A few outgoing scarlet capes were moving along the path towards the gates. It was not only the boy's father who was cheered. The others also felt hope in the air, though it was mixed with ice. They were anxious that it should not melt too quickly.

On the stroke of three the swing doors burst open and were fastened against brass hinges on either side. They were being beckoned in by a familiar, smiling nurse. But the man stayed behind talking with the woman for a few minutes longer. He was telling her something and it was easy enough to guess what was happening. He was no more telling it to her than he was telling it to the fire extinguisher. He was simply rehearsing in detail what he would tell his son.

'Yesterday afternoon,' he was saying, 'I'd no sooner got in than my neighbours came round for a chat, and to tell me about their latest bed-and-breakfast. They do it summer and winter—have done for years. And do you know who this latest man turns out to be? A first-class chef turned preacher. Imagine it. He'd been giving people a great deal of pleasure, no doubt, whipping up the soufflés and concocting recipes à la Robertson or whatever his name is. And now ... ! Not only that, but he can't leave well alone. He's got to go round condemning his former job. Condemning it! Oh, that some of our present preachers would turn Sunday chefs! Would that not give us a more digestible day?'

They had now started to move through the swing doors but his voice came after her. 'And so I see this architect on TV last night is proposing a floating city. I like the idea. Do you like the idea?' Yes, she said, she liked it very much indeed.

'I've forgotten how it would work, but every window would have this magnificent changing view. How about that?'

'Yes, wonderful,' said the woman. But she kept moving on because they had to be rather strict about time here and the hour passed quickly.

'But I'm not so sure,' his voice pursued her, 'about the sort of city that goes a mile up into the sky.' This time she didn't turn round and wasn't meant to. His eyes were already fixed on the passage to the left and on a door at the far end of it. Her own route took her up a flight of stairs and along a corridor on the other side. They parted abruptly as they always did, he to the left and she to the right.

It happened that they met again in the evening at the seven to eight visiting hour. For some time back they had come in on both afternoon and evening visits, though they did the double shift for different reasons—the man because his son was very ill, the woman because her daughter was almost well. It seemed the two extremes demanded most. For the second time that day they stood at the plate glass windows staring across. But the transformation from afternoon to evening was always spectacular. In place of solid buildings were row upon row of incandescent light cubes set in blackness, giving a vision which was almost clair-voyant into the rooms opposite. Here and there among the white cubes were a few dim rooms lit by blue, and visitors tended to stare at these with particular intensity as though the distant blue rooms held the secret of life and death— a secret being unaccountably withheld from themselves. Tonight, however, brightness came from the ground as well as the walls. Even the skimpy trees spiked with snow looked theatrical. On the bowling-green the line of the heart showed up thicker and clearer than before.

As usual, the man and the woman arrived early, and after their first few comments, they fell silent. It was not a vast silence but the woman decided it was too long for com-fort. They did not know one another well enough for this. She had also become accustomed to the non-silence policy of the hospital. This was not made too obvious but it could be felt. When necessary a good deal of chatter, not to say clatter, covered certain black pits of feeling. Even the brisk rattle of curtain rails round an emotion was better than nothing. The woman could chatter herself when she had a mind to.

'If the forecast's anything to go by it's to be colder than ever,' she said. 'But no more snow meantime. Well, thank goodness for that. The bus had the worst time ever on that hill tonight. There was one moment I thought we'd all be out on the road pushing. What's your opinion of double-deckers on a hill like that? Last year there were letters to the paper. Do you think double-deckers are dangerous on that particular stretch?' The man nodded but gave no opinion, so she answered for him. 'Yes, they *are* more dangerous and not just in snow—in a wind too.

51

In a high wind they can pitch and swing like a ship at sea.' Again there was silence as they stared ahead. The woman took courage from the brilliant patches of light below. 'What did your son think of the cook?' she asked, smiling. The man unfocused his gaze reluctantly. His eyebrows indicated a complete noncomprehension. 'The chef turning preacher,' said the woman with still unfaltering brightness.

'Oh *that*.' He waved it impatiently aside. 'Absolutely nothing. It didn't interest him at all. There was nothing to it, of course.' The woman could have stopped there. She was virtually being invited to take no interest in anything herself. But she felt the need to go further. 'The floating city—what does he make of that idea? If it doesn't sound ludicrous to put it that way—isn't it his line of country?'

'He hardly heard it. He thought it scarcely worth while listening.'

The woman looked down quickly and started to rearrange some of the things in her bag, but a moment later she was startled by his tense voice, suddenly much louder. 'There *was* one thing he took up. *One* thing he listened to. He took great exception to my mention of the heart.' The woman stopped rustling in her bag and took a quick look down at it. She had almost forgotten it was there.

'Never again!' said the man. 'What a mistake to talk about outside things. How stupid I've become. How thick!'

'But what happened?'

'Nothing—except he worked himself into a fury. And don't think,' said the man as though picking her up, 'don't think he'll forget it. I know my son. He's going to lie there and meditate on hearts and the people who draw hearts.'

Sometimes the doors would be opened for early visitors. It happened this evening. At least fifteen minutes before time the friendly nurse came through and wedged them back. She noticed that this pair were tired and that the cold glass where they leaned had taken colour from their cheeks. They looked deserving of comfort, of some privilege for themselves. But whatever it was they didn't take it. They acknowledged the open door but remained where they were.

'Who are they then?' said the woman. 'Who are these people who draw hearts?'

'Vandals!' the man cried. 'And no different from any other kind. So he says. Secret vandals!' They both stared at the bowling-green, the woman in some surprise, the man with bitterness. 'Oh yes,' he said, 'harmless *this* time. That he admits. But whoever could do that could do it in much worse and lasting ways. It's the brand-new hearts chiselled on standing stones he's thinking of, hearts dug out of trees and slashed across pillars. He's seen himself a hideous double heart complete with dates and arrows branded on a temple wall. Can you blame him? Buildings are his job. Oh, it's not only hearts! He is thinking of every effacement he ever set eyes on. And I set him off!'

'It will melt,' said the woman who could think of nothing better to say.

'But not from his mind,' said the man. 'I know my son.' He turned and walked quickly away through the open door. The woman waited on for a bit. She felt she was getting to know the young man too. And she had to admit that with the best will in the world she didn't absolutely care for the sound of him. Had never in fact cared. On the whole her opinion was that illness made neither devils nor angels. She took the view that it brought out and perhaps exaggerated what was already there. From what she had heard, there was and always had been a born complainer there. Long before his illness he had complained. She had never seen him and she was exceedingly sorry for him. She was sorry for any obsessions he might have. But she was not, she was thankful to say, obliged to like him.

She didn't see the father next day. But on the following afternoon they met in the corridor. It was colder than ever—colder if possible than on the last few days. Not a scrap of snow had melted or shifted. On the trees the snow blossoms had set like icing sugar. The heart on the bowling-green had not altered its shape by a single ice crystal. It was clear when the man spoke that his son had not altered his views either. He was preoccupied with vandalism. It had been no good trying to change the subject. The boy had kept an irritable silence before bursting out in the same vein. They had not mentioned the heart again, but it was the basis of the business. And the vandalism had broadened to include all spoilings in country as well as city, past damage and damage to come.

'Is it so strange?' said the father. 'He's an architect, isn't he? As far as he's concerned nothing in its final shape comes up to what was planned. Everything falls short. Just now he exaggerates. Yes. But he was always like that. His expectations are high.'

'I'm sure,' said the woman quickly.

'A perfectionist.'

'Yes, of course he is!'

'And such people can be reminded, can be irritated by things which the rest of us ...'

'Oh, I know that!' she exclaimed. The man looked exhausted with the effort of explanation. He took a deep breath before saying:

'But I've a feeling this evening will be different. We'll get off the subject. Why not? It was an accident that it ever got into the picture at all. He *will* forget.' He dropped his eyes to the bowling-green. They both stared at the heart. Engraved as it was out of a substance which might vanish at any instant, it had kept its shape. It seemed innocent and at the same time bold—a peaceful, yet a childishly stubborn shape. In the absence of initials, arrows, prints of any kind, there was no message to be read. But emptiness gave it power. It was no longer strange. Already it was part of the surroundings. It was a harmonious shape, and the woman decided it was benign. But she wondered how the man saw it now. As a deliberate disfigurement? A shape, meaningless and gross, perhaps, set there to try the endurance of his son and himself.

It had begun to snow slightly again at the evening visiting hour, but the corridor was crowded as usual for Saturday was a popular day for family visits. There were plenty of new faces and tonight even the regulars were in good form. The snow had put fight into them. They were not prepared to make a mystery out of this building. It was something to get in from the cold, and they expressed some envy for the patients in their snug beds. There came a point when even illness must be kept in its place. There was a big difference between being alive and being dead and it had better not be forgotten. At any rate, ribaldry, in place of awe, was long overdue in the place. It was a night for comparing fat and thin sisters, for stripping doctors of the laundered coat. Surgeons were scrutinized as either wilder than the wildest maniac or staid as councillors, and the immaculate matron in her virgin pie-ruff must be sacrificed to one or other of them before the night was out. There were few doctors around just now. It was not the time for doctors. But when one did appear as though by accident, going slowly past looking neither to right nor left, the relatives stared boldly after him. They were controlling the desire to spring forward and wrench an answer out of him—an explanation, a diagnosis, or even a plain yes or no. The stray doctor was aware of this. He kept his eyes fixed on a distant mark at the end of the corridor in an effort to maintain dignity and keep his footing on the spotless floor when on every side the endlessly questioning eyes threatened to topple him up.

The young man's father was not among the earliest arrivals tonight. He came on the dot of seven and disappeared immediately in the direction of the wards. This time the woman was ahead of him but she looked back once and got a quick response. He waved. His smile was cheerful, as though he'd quickly caught the mood of the evening and had no intention of being odd man out. The woman waited for him in the corridor when the hour was up. It was not an evening for formalities or reserve.

'And how was he?' she asked at once as he came up. 'Did you manage to get off that subject?'

'No,' he said, 'I did not. And we are back to square one.'

'The bowling-green?'

'Oh, I thought *that* at any rate was over and done with. But he'd thought of something else. How am I to put it to you?'

'Tell me then.'

'He was upset, to put it mildly, brooding now on the fact that the heart down there has nothing inside it, none of the usual appendages. No words or signs. Not a mark. If it's to be properly denounced it must conform, and this one has not come up to expectation. It says nothing. It gives nothing. It is not even a lasting blot on the landscape. This empty heart is not enough for him it seems!' The man had forgotten to subdue his voice to the required hospital mildness. It got louder as he went on and ended on a note of pain. One or two people glanced sympathetically at him in passing. One or two looked annoyed. He had become a threat to the hard-won mood of cheer.

The woman didn't move or speak for a long time. She was looking straight in front of her out of the window. It was still snowing and there was a slight wind. It was hard to see how the fine flakes would ever touch ground. At one moment they formed spirals in the air and at another, slanting lines which shifted, or on sudden gusts blew upward higher and higher until the widely separating flakes disappeared into darkness overhead. All the same, the thin layer of snow had already altered things below. The two lines of footsteps on the bowling-green were almost obliterated. The centre of the heart, shining in the light from the hospital windows, was softly padded out with new white snow. It still proclaimed itself, but gently. Now that even the footsteps were gone, this smoothing and rounding had given it a feeling of completeness and an absolute calm.

'Do you know,' said the woman, rousing herself at last to speak. 'I think I shall put it to my daughter—your son's problem, I mean. Just as a matter of interest I'd like her opinion. How would that be?'

'Certainly. Please tell her anything you like,' said the man politely.

'In my opinion she's got insight as well as common sense.'

'I'm sure,' said the man, keeping himself from moving off with an effort.

'And then, of course, she is young herself.'

The man answered by making a weary obeisance in the direction of the wards. It was done without irony. He acknowledged youth while admitting that he himself was absolutely played out. Finished. Right now there was only one thing he wanted and that was to get home. He had talked so much about his son, however, and asked so little about her daughter it was up to him to stay on the spot. But the woman was moving off herself. 'Then I'll see you tomorrow,' she said.

Their meeting next day came at the end of the afternoon visit. It seemed casual, almost accidental. The woman was standing at the window with her back to the light, studying herself in a small handbag mirror. The absorbed, disapproving regard of the middle-aged woman for her own face disappeared as he came up. But she turned back for one more caustic glance at her left cheek.

'Well, I've seen my daughter,' she said, forcing the mirror back into her handbag's jungle. 'She thought about it for a long time. And I may say she has the greatest sympathy for your son's point of view. Indeed she shares it. She understood perfectly his irritation, his frustration ... But as for the heart—well, she takes a more straightforward view of that. Why worry? Why fuss about what is or isn't inside it? It was never meant, she says, to have letters, words, signs, or anything else. That is not the style of the thing. On the other hand, it is not an *empty* heart.'

'No?' said the man.

'I'm simply repeating her words,' the woman said, looking at him impatiently for the first time. '*Not* an empty heart, but an open one. For anyone and everyone. One can take it or leave it, but there it is. It is fabulous, she says. It is fantastic. It is an outsize super-heart. And there is absolutely nothing more to be said about it.'

The man said nothing more about it, but he thought for a long time. 'I shall pass on the message,' he said at last, bowing his head, '... and how on earth I will manage ...'

'You'll make nothing of it, I hope.'

'I'll certainly try to make it nothing. I am tempted to scoff a bit at your daughter's view.'

'Oh, she's tough enough to take it! In that way—your son and my daughter—aren't they both tough enough? And that they've never met and never will meet has absolutely nothing to do with it. They stand together.'

'Indeed I hope so,' said the man. He turned quickly away and went on past her towards the stair.

Next day the woman was occupied with other visitors to her daughter. He saw her only in passing. But they met briefly the following day at the end of the evening visit. It was hot in the corridor. The woman was complaining about the tightness of her snowboots on the thick rubber floor. The radiators at the window were scorching, and visitors emerging from lemonade-filled wards complained of thirst. Beyond the swing doors one or two women patients were already wandering about in open, flowery dressing-gowns. The nurses looked warm and pink as sun-bathers. Tonight the hospital was like a huge, hot ocean liner, stranded in ice.

'So our promised thaw has not come after all,' said the woman.

'I can't say it worries me one way or the other,' the man replied. The woman looked at him quickly and was encouraged by something in his expression. She waited for a bit and getting no further response said:

'And your son. Is *he* reconciled ... to the snow?'

'Reconciled? Never! That is not his way. He reconciles himself to nothing. He takes his own view and always will. If he does change his mind he must think it all out for himself—through it and round and over it.'

'Of course, of course,' said the woman. 'But what is his view—of that?'

The man looked in the direction of the bowling-green and away again. Yet the woman was still encouraged by something about him. She was now reduced to pointing directly down at the heart. The man consented to look at it again but said nothing. He was stubborn like his son.

'Oh well then,' said the woman. 'What is *your* view of it?'

The man shrugged his shoulders and glanced down. He considered it as though measuring it, as though matching it up against all other possible shapes.

'Oh—the size of that thing!' he exclaimed at last. 'The extravagance! Isn't it a regular pantomime piece ...?'

'Yes, yes,' agreed the woman, and waited.

The man shook his head as though finished with what he had to say. Nevertheless he put down the bag he was carrying and opened his arms wide, bringing them slowly together again into a circle with only the tips of his fingers joined. For an instant he enfolded the empty space in front of him. He demonstrated an almost imperceptible capture, an embrace.

'It is a not unfriendly shape,' the man said, dropping his arms and picking up his bag again.

But the woman seemed perfectly satisfied with these words. At once she began to move away from the window, taking care to do it with the least possible fuss or disturbance to the man looking down on the bowling-green. As she was a large woman and rather clumsy, it was not easy. It was a case of drawing on her gloves without moving her elbows, of sorting out a complication of handbag and carrier-bag straps while pulling down her helmet shaped cap over her ears. She managed not to open her mouth again. She didn't look in his direction. Padded with clothes, strapped and helmeted, like a diver she moved, silently, in rubber boots over the rubber floor. Slowly, cautiously— yet with some hint of deep-sea buoyancy in her gait—she drifted off.

House-Hunter

The house-hunter had looked over five empty houses in the last two hours. At the door of the sixth, in late afternoon, he met a woman at the same game. She was staring eagerly up at the FOR SALE notice protruding over a window in the top flat of the building. 'Then we can go up together?' she said. If an identical set of agent's keys had given her this fellow feeling, the man couldn't subscribe to it. He was tired, not looking for company, but there was nothing for it but to nod and start climbing. This was a city of stairs and in particular it was a district of steep, dingy stairs with elegant banisters lit only at the top by elaborate glass cupolas which had illumined better days. It became brighter as they climbed, but not much brighter. Still, they were not far from the sea. At the very top, while the woman tried the key in the door, the man stood and watched a great seagull shape, and then another, glide across the glass overhead—shadows merely, for the glass was opaque with decades of soot and droppings. Now the woman had opened the door with a smile and a flourish, and they stepped inside. There was not much to smile about. Darkness and a musty smell. A forbidding hall of closed doors, and a floor of creaking, black-painted boards over which they moved quietly as though fearful of stirring up life in a dead place. The door on the left took them

62

into a kitchen and there they stood, the woman looking about the room, and the man, who with one glance had removed the house from his list, taking his chance to look at the woman.

She was tall and dark, with an angular clumsiness of movement which took away from the confidence of her strong arms, her large well-shaped hands and feet. Her shoulders were broad and slightly stooping. She was middle-aged, handsome enough, but with something of the tatty crow about her. Once perhaps she'd been sprung for some flight or feat of strength—ready, long ago, for the get-away. This urgency had all gone and in its place was a strange and artificial eagerness.

'It's cheerful enough anyway,' she said, glancing through the long window at a red sun going down between strips of dark cloud. Almost close enough to put their arms around was a row of forbidding chimney-pots and beyond that a sharp grey spire set between two sheer slopes of slate.

'But not cheerful enough for me!' said the man. 'Better not bother about the view until we've examined the floor. One of them, they say, isn't absolutely sound. Would it be this one?' He tramped around for a while lifting up patches of linoleum and stamping on loose boards with his heel. With his toe he kicked at the wainscoting below the window, wedged up a splinter and put his fingers down into the crack. He traced a scar in the wall above the fireplace, opened the door of the larder and sniffed with distaste the smell of dust and grease mixed with a touch of fruitiness. He examined the shelves, moved a left-over, cracked dish, noted dark rings on the wood, came out again and pointed at a corner of the ceiling where there was a suspicious patch of flaking plaster. The woman watched. She made him feel—without moving or speaking and still with something friendly in her gaze—that he was spoiling an occasion.

'When you've looked at as many as I have you learn to leave nothing, absolutely nothing to chance,' he remarked, defending himself from the look. 'And then, of course, I'll have to give a blow by blow account to my family—every stick and stone, every nail and screw, every splinter, crack, hole and spot in the place before they'll deign to come and see for themselves. That's the kind of family I have. What about yours?' He was made to regret having even approached a personal question. Her face immediately changed. She turned and stared with passion at the flaking patch, then studied the crack in the floor, grimaced at the cupboard behind him as though appalled at its sourness, and finally let her eyes fall to her own feet which she examined with a momentary hostility which he felt could only have been meant for his face.

Together they left the kitchen, but silently, under a cloud—though how or why it had come the man had no idea. He wandered on by himself for a while, out into the dark hall and back, then opened the door adjoining the kitchen into a living-room. Here was another state of things altogether. A place so completely different that it had no connection at all with the kitchen or the petty and inexplicable misunderstandings that had occurred there. The room was a place of pure fantasy.

'Come here!' the house-hunter called across to the woman where she still stood in the hall. 'You'll enjoy this!'

She came slowly over and stood beside him. The room was a large one with long windows looking down onto bare, walled courtyards below. There were no gardens down there—not a scrap of grass or leaf to be seen. But the room made up for it. Somebody had done his best to turn it into a forest with fruit and vegetables thrown in for good measure. The place was lined from floor to cornice with a patterned paper of thin black tree trunks, terminating around the top of the walls in a broad band of interlocking branches. It was the sort of paper which might pass in a banqueting-hall. In a smaller room it became a thicket. 'And look up there!' he exclaimed, pointing. In well-kept houses of this city it was the habit to paint the cornices as white as icing sugar—whether the design was fruits, leaves, scrolls or egg-shapes. The unidentified fruits of this particular one had been painted in blue, purple and red with here and there a touch of dark green on leaves and scrolls. There was some highlighting on the fruit. Above it all the ceiling loomed in dark thundery blue. 'A monsoon room,' the man groaned, pretending to ease his collar. 'And down there!' Here and there at the foot of the tree-trunks, looking like a child's schoolroom frieze, spikes of grass, some cabbagy leaves and a few crude fern shapes had been painted in by hand. Shelving had been put up against one wall, like a flimsy fencing set waist-high against the trees. It was a rickety contraption tacked together with cheap wood in a series of boxes so shallow it was difficult to imagine what sort of things could have been set there. Not books, certainly—not cups or dishes. Only the smallest objects. Or perhaps nothing.

'What do you make of it?' said the house-hunter. 'Could you imagine yourself moving in here? Cutting through this vegetation. Removal men wouldn't be enough. A lumberman would be more like it!'

She remained grave, still on her dignity, as though a smile might unfix her. If she was surprised by this forest she was determined not to show it.

'Well, it's just paper after all. You'd have no difficulty

stripping the place. For the rest ...' She glanced at the fruity cornice, at the stormy ceiling. '... it's a business of repainting, if you wanted to make the change.'

'If I *wanted*! If we moved in—which heaven forbid—we'd change the house from top to bottom. The only thing is ...' She waited expectantly. 'Even when you'd changed every scrap, even after you'd scraped and gutted and scrubbed, repainted and furnished. Even then ...'

'What then?' She looked apprehensive.

'You'd still have the people to contend with.'

'The people?' She was shaken out of her calm this time.

'Or person, I mean. Whoever lived here. They'd leave an atmosphere behind, wouldn't they? No amount of hammering or papering could get rid of that!'

But the woman stepped suddenly past him to the window. The movement was abrupt and her elbow sent the agent's paper flying from his hand. She made no apology. He continued to examine the room in silence. In silence she stared down at the grey yards below. He had almost forgotten about her and was bending to examine some blue butterfly tiling round the fireplace when she spoke again.

'What exactly have you *against* colour?'

'Nothing. Nor, of course, against trees or fruit, flowers or vegetables—in their place.'

'Oh, I see.'

'A wood has to *be* a wood. And a room a room. Let's just say I like my trees outside. Even my sky. I like my blue sky outside and not in.'

'I see, I see.' Was the voice sarcastic?

After a bit he joined her at the window. They were looking out at a sky which was a spacious, even grey—not an unusual sight in the city at any time of the year. And everything in sight underneath it was grey except for two scarlet tins studding an overflowing ash-bucket in the yard below. Beyond that the houses and smoke, backdoors and lanes, garages and brokendown cars—all were grey. The outlook was uniformly dismal as could be. In the face of it the house-hunter felt a passing shiver of sympathy for the wild wallpaper. But there were limits. 'The room's a bit of a nightmare,' he said, stepping back. 'At best you could call it a rather mad dream.'

'And that down there. What would you call *that*?' she asked.

'That's nothing. It's nameless. Just empty space made into a dump. It's sheer bad planning, if you want to put the blame somewhere.'

'Mad planning,' she murmured.

'I said "bad".'

He wandered slowly round and out of the room again, vaguely put out by their exchange. Next door in the bathroom some artificial flowers had been left behind—two waxy red roses with wired stems wound around the toothbrush holder and a bunch of papery daisies fixed to the corner of the mirror. The windows here were unusually high and narrow and the lower panes had been made obscure by bands of blue and green fishes and cut-out weed fronds stuck to the glass. Steam and dusting had reduced them and there were worn patches which he could see through as though staring out of a fishy, summer sea clear up into the grey, winter air above. He moved on into a bedroom. He sensed silver. It was difficult to put a finger on it for the window was small and the place dark, but a faint phosphorescence came from the walls. Closer inspection showed the facing wall was covered with squared-off dark paper, each square containing one full moon and a dusting of stars. On the ceiling paper the stars were very small indeed—merely a mass of white specks—as though the owner had intended the roof to dissolve into the most distant part of the sky. Half a curtain of spangly stuff still hung at the window and the sill was stuck with a starry mosaic of silvery paper. Only the yellow shade left hanging from the ceiling, spiked like sun or sunflower, stood out from the night designs. The house-hunter was examining this with a smile when her voice came from behind.

'Why should you bother with it all seeing you'd never think to buy the place—not in a month of Sundays?'

'For the same reason as yourself, I suppose. Curiosity. I'm curious to see how people live.'

'You'll not find out much by staring at left-over lampshades, will you?' she replied with unexpected sharpness.

'Not much,' he said, 'except that this must have hung over the bed. They'd snap off the sun at night. In the morning they'd wake up and stare at it. She, or perhaps he, must have made it. Where could you buy a shade like that? And how did they manage to leave such an object behind?'

'Oh, so you've even worked out there were two of them, have you?'

'There are marks of a double bed—there and there.' He pointed them out on the wall.

'Clever. But did nobody ever sleep alone in a double bed before? Maybe it's a tenement of widows. Maybe a whole streetful. Women have a way of living on, you see. You've noticed that?'

She walked slowly away from him. She looked somehow proud, and yet at the same time lightweight—with one step showing dignity and with the next a lack of balance. He decided it was a matter of uneven floorboards. For some

68

time they were separate, and went about their business silently. When they passed one another again in the room of trees the man felt compelled to murmur: 'Whoever it was lived here—one, two, or a dozen of them—I wouldn't care to meet them on a dark night!' Again they separated, and for a longer time. But finally he came back to the kitchen and sat waiting for her. There was no need for him to do this. He had seen all he wanted to see and more. And he was not committed to seeing her ever again. From her expression as he'd passed her in the living-room she might have been glad enough if she'd never set eyes on him. Yet still he waited.

Outside the grey was deeper. The spire of the church was bent and blunted in mist, but its bell clanged the hour. Five o'clock. He had no business to be sitting there. Long before this the keys should have gone back to the agent's office. He could imagine other house-hunters waiting impatiently for them, finally giving up and going home with an angry vision of some fine, cheerful flat they had missed. He sat on. He heard the woman moving from the bedroom to the bathroom, round the hall, and back to the living-room. There were intervals of absolute silence. What was she thinking? Did she still resent his presence or was she glad of company? After a while he forgot the house and thought only of the woman. It began to grow in his mind that before they finally separated he must come to terms with her, though exactly what the phrase meant in these circumstances he had no idea. It was cold now and his position on the metal kerb beside the empty grate reminded him of it. Outside on the common stair the sound of an occasional passing footstep made the empty house still more silent. But at last he heard the woman coming towards the kitchen. She entered quietly without a glance

69

in his direction. But the house-hunter stared at her. Over her arm was folded the spangled half curtain. She had the plastic flowers from the bathroom in her hand. Still ignoring him she came over to the left of the fireplace, carefully untied a pencil which was hanging from a piece of string on a hook, and put it in her pocket. She crossed to the sink and for a moment hovered over a left-over bottle of cleaning fluid, thought better of it and went over to the window where she stood for a moment examining the cloth over her arm.

The house-hunter's carefully planned remarks were forgotten. All the time, then, there had been a scavenger in these dismal rooms. The proud woman with the ambiguous step had succumbed, and crashingly, to the lightweight. Would she remove the bunch of safety-pins on the window ledge? Had she missed the bit of soap—almost new—at the top of the bath? Not all the loot would be as easy as that. She was going to need help if she wanted the lampshade.

'Why shouldn't I?' she demanded, turning suddenly and catching his expression. The fierceness of it made him jump.

'No reason at all.' He avoided the eyes defiantly staring into his.

'Why shouldn't I?' she asked again, her eyes flashing. 'I *made* these curtains!' They confronted one another silently for a second, both outraged, both staring at some chasm that had opened up between them. Anger saved the man. 'You could have told me it was your house!' he exclaimed.

'*Is*—is my house. It's not sold yet!' she at once replied. She put her bag on the floor, crossed the room and disappeared into the deep cupboard, coming out again with

70

the cracked blue dish. Ignoring the man, she ran her eyes over the fireplace, picked up an old poker before deciding against it, and went back to her bag. She kept the single curtain over her arm.

'And why not?' she asked again, swinging round to stare. 'Every single thing is mine!' She did up her coat, picked up her bag and walked out into the hall. The house-hunter was nothing now. But he followed her.

'Look—I'm appalled if anything I've said ...!'

'Don't bother.'

'If you'd given me one hint—do you imagine I'd *ever* ...!'

'Oh, I don't want to hear about it.' She had her hand on the front door.

'Then I'd better come too. We can go together. As we came.'

'Oh no!' There was outrage in her protest. The house-hunter watched her go down two flights of stairs and cautiously followed after. Halfway down the next she looked up. 'You scare me,' she said. 'No heart. You really frighten me. And I can tell you one thing.' She lifted her arm and for one moment stared up at him through the piece of spangled stuff. 'I wouldn't like to meet *you* on a dark night.' Whether by this gesture she hid her own face or spared his own—the house-hunter was not to know. She dropped her arm and went down the bottom flight. He saw her fold the curtain into her bag before making for the outer door. She seemed to grasp the door calmly enough, but between its opening swing and its crashing close a chilling, gritty dust from the street reached up and struck his cheek.

The Colour

Mr Garrad had rung rather late in the day—some time after tea when the disorder had shown itself. But it wasn't as late as all that, and anyway they'd had it in writing that in an emergency someone could always come right away. It was urgent all right—not something to be cured at home by a bit of tinkering and on-the-spot treatment. It was not the first time it had happened either. Garrad looked pained when he came back from the phone. His wife sat on the sofa nursing a pillow for comfort. She knew instinctively it would be a comfortless evening. The son and daughter had emerged from their bedrooms and hung limply on the banister to hear the diagnosis.

'They will come this evening,' said Garrad sitting down at the other end of the sofa, 'and they will do something about it, if possible.' That was the devil of it—the 'if possible' which sounded the dirge on hope. How many 'if possibles' had these two not heard—and yet weren't used to it yet.

'If possible?' muttered his wife as though testing out a foreign phrase in her mouth.

'That's it. I'm giving you their word for word.' They sat in silence. 'What will you do then? Will you go out?' said the wife after a bit.

'I'll wait till they come. *If* they come. Then I'll go out.'

They waited fifty minutes until, as by a miracle, two young men turned up. The family watched them as they knelt and tested and talked together. Nothing came of it. All the others could see was the odd red streak that made the heart jump till they saw it was only the reflection of the bus-stop sign on the other side of the street. The men answered Garrad's questions. They were very young. But it wasn't their age that bothered him. It was their politeness, their gentleness. They had the cheerful gentleness of stretcher-bearers on a serious case as they lifted the set in their arms and carried it out. This same pair had actually put in the colour. Now, for the second time, they were taking it away. 'How long this time?' Garrad asked as they went past him, carefully manoeuvring it round the corner of the passage and shielding it from the sharp edge of the hall table. They shook their heads and smiled. He watched them go through the front door, careful not to jolt or trip. He watched the colour being carried further and further away until it finally disappeared into the waiting van.

'Well, that's that!' he cried coming back, falsely cheerful, into the living-room.

'Nobody minds a couple of nights without,' said his wife. 'But there's Friday. It's Friday I'm thinking about.'

'And Sunday,' he added. On Friday there was a thriller serial two episodes from the end. There was also a cookery demonstration which they all watched hungrily week by week, never mind whether they'd had their meal or not. They were hungry for the colour of this food—the familiar yellow yolks of eggs being broken into scarlet bowls, white cream poured into chocolate sauce, and all stirred with a blue spoon. In the background tomatoes were piled against aubergines, polished to ebony—on the side, platters of apples, grapes and oranges. Now and then the demonstrator would wipe her hands on an apron striped green and blue. Garrad's wife was a good cook herself. She used milk and eggs. She could have got a scarlet bowl if she'd wanted it. She'd have been the first to admit that her milk was whiter, the eggs yellower than the screen ones. But that was not the point. Where was the comfort in it? For Garrad, who liked the country, there was a regular Sunday series of different landscapes filmed hour by hour from dawn to moonrise, showing the changing colours of sky, field and river throughout one day. The colour was not bad, in Garrad's estimation. It was as real as you could get unless you actually had the thing behind you in the window. Yes, they'd done a good job on colour and the chances were it would get better as time went on.

'You're going out then?' said his wife.

'Might just as well.' He stepped out into the street, into a warm autumn evening. His own street was made up of small modern houses with long gardens, well-known in the district for their new-planted trees. Most people were tending a sapling. Garrad was proud of this himself but this evening he had no eyes for the spindly branches beside him. In spite of himself he kept looking up at the TV aerials growing overhead, frail-looking yet tough enough to withstand the most ferocious blast. Not a house without these magic roof-twigs. All the same he was the only man for a long way round these parts who had colour. The first man. A kind of Adam of the new vision. Very soon—perhaps in a year or so, possibly in a few months, they'd all have it. But he was the first. He strode along quickly at first, then gradually more and more slowly as the first fury of his frustration spent itself. He was able to smile at the few persons he knew who were sitting at windows or working in their gardens along the street. At one or two he stopped. A married couple he knew rather better than the rest were out staring at a bed of roses and Garrad stopped and stared too.

'You're out early,' the man remarked, stepping across the bed towards him.

'Yes. Good to get a breath of air after the office.'

'And the wife?'

'Fine. Or not bad is more like it. She gets easily put out, thrown off her stroke ...'

'But she's well?'

'She worries.'

'Like the rest of us. And yourself?'

'All right. Rather dull, as you see.'

'Sorry to hear your wife has worries,' said the woman. 'Not serious ones, I hope.'

'Nothing much. It's the colour trouble again. Have you thought about colour yourself?'

They immediately stripped themselves of all frivolity, let go of the roses. 'Colour? I may say we read and listen to everything that's being said on that particular issue,' the man said. 'I think you know my views on the colour question.'

'It wasn't that though. It's colour TV I'm talking about.'

'Oh, I see. No, I've no views on that, I'm afraid. Not yet. Haven't got the money to have any views on that at the moment. Now, this colour question. As I said before—I think you know my views on that.'

'Certainly I know them. I share them.'

'I hope you do.'

'That's a queer way to put it, and not particularly complimentary to Mr Garrad here,' said his wife coming nearer. 'You're implying he may have prejudices of one

75

kind or another or that he's afraid to come out with them.'

'That's utter nonsense! But there *is* a queer thing. Here we all are airing our views about colour, with lowered voices. Some day, looking back, the world will think it's unbelievably ludicrous. We'll be all colours and thankful to be. It'll be a disgrace to be pure white, pure black, brown or yellow. That's how it'll be in the world to come.'

'In a future world you mean,' said his wife.

'The same.'

'Because "world to come" usually means "next life". Which is a very different matter.'

'I have no views about a next life, none whatever. Except there's said to be no marriage or giving in marriage and that's all that interests me.'

'So you can see where your colour views get us,' said his wife to Garrad. 'I hope your wife doesn't get what I have to put up with. And by the way, what about a bunch of roses to take back?'

'Lovely,' said Garrad quickly. 'Lovely. But I'll get them on the way back if it's all the same ...'

He moved on past other gardens competing in brightness and neatness, past doors painted blue, white and green, down to the busy corner and round it and on towards that part which grew more and more congested near the crossing of main roads but where, miraculously, on clear days, in a minute closed-in wedge between a pub and a church, you could just see the blue line of distant sea. When he was a young man Garrad had cherished this almost invisible wedge of the town. There was some fractional romance about it which he occasionally remembered nowadays when he was struggling through the rush-hour crowds or waiting in longer and longer queues. There was sometimes a pin-pointing of clouds over this sea, now and then the fleck of a ship. Sometimes it was no more than the narrow dazzle of light between black brick. He seldom looked for it now. When he looked he seldom saw it. Twenty more years of traffic had nearly obscured it. A smart addition to the church and a new signboard on the pub had pared it to an even smaller piece of sea and sky. He went further and further in towards the centre and slowly out again on the other side where most of the town's public buildings stood—banks, town hall, libraries and Technical College—all with a sizeable bit of green in front. He came to the main modern school with its huge glass frontage where you could look right into empty classrooms and corridors and see flowers blazing along the sills, and maps, mobiles, posters on the opposite walls. A late janitor strolled up to the gates as he went past. 'Ah ... the young devils ... they're in luck, aren't they?' Garrad said. 'They're never done looking. They can see the whole world go past as they do their sums. When I think how we had to fix our eyes on a two feet by three block of blackboard. There wasn't anywhere else to look. What wouldn't we have given to see all this!'

'But would you say it was a *good* thing?' said the janitor, leaning his elbow on a spike of railing.

'I was just coming to that. Is it?' said Garrad. 'Does it help them concentrate? Does it help them choose what things to look at out of all the stuff going past the window? Does it make them selective? S e l e c t i v e!' Garrad rolled and relished the word on his tongue. The janitor took his elbows off the spike. 'And these are going too.'

'What's that?'

'The spikes are going.'

'Well that's good I suppose. No spikes, eh? All this and spikeless too. Makes you wonder how *we* came through at

77

all at their age.' He walked on gravely, passing one or two acquaintances on his way. He made this distinction with middle-age. Real friends got fewer and fewer while acquaintances grew and multiplied. These days he used the word 'real' a lot. Real. He hung on grimly to reality like an acrobat with a metal plug between the teeth hanging over a void. Real friends, real food, real entertainment, real service, real flavour, real bread, real leather, real hair, real love, real money, real women. They were all whizzing away from him. Some things he'd missed out. Real colour. It was not yet added to his list.

It was cooler now and the street quieter. At another crossing of streets a miniature market was packing up its stalls. Men and women, untying aprons blotched with juice, were getting ready to heave up piles of empty crates onto lorries or into their own shops behind, while round about a few left-over baskets of battered fruit were being fingered by late-comers. A few stalls were still intact. One was slung round like an Arabian tent with purple and crimson cloth, overhung by long red and blue nylon dresses with flowered sashes. Rows of boots, dangling from their laces round the top of the stall, kicked half-heartedly in the breeze as though engaged in some mild, disembodied game of football.

A couple who were hurrying past stopped suddenly beside Garrad. They were coming from their shop where, over a long time-span of changing fashions, every single object there had changed from junk to antique and back to junk again. They kept their spirits up. 'Hullo Mr Garrad. Very thoughtful you look. Are you contemplating the skating boots up there or what?' asked the husband.

'Well I might yet. Right now I'm only out for a stroll.'

'Good. But don't forget to be back for seven, will you?'

'Seven. What's that?'

'What's seven! Don't tell me you were thinking of giving a miss to the last of the Great Gardens?'

'I've no choice. It's broken down on us.' Garrad told the tale again. Of how colour was brought and taken back, and brought and taken back again. He didn't fuss—simply told it with a wry smile while they exclaimed in sympathy. But they were still leaning at a steep angle towards home. 'So we'd have been better to stay with plain black and white for a while,' Garrad went on. 'That way we'd never have known what we were missing.'

'Do you think so?' Their faces lost a little sympathy. They had no colour. Garrad knew he'd been tactless.

'It's just,' he said, 'that it doesn't take long to get used to colour.'

'I suppose so,' said the wife. 'Do you find it true?'

'True?'

'Yes, I believe it varies a lot. Some say they'll never get it true to life.'

'Well it's different of course.'

'They're never going to get it absolutely true. That's what I heard.'

'I wouldn't say never. It depends what you mean by true. It's going to get better and better.'

'Does anything?' said the man. 'I'm afraid I'm a pessimist. And I'm rather odd about colour. I don't believe I'd like it unless it was absolutely true. I suppose it's because you could call me a bit of an artist. Isn't that right, Cath?'

'That's right,' said his wife without enthusiasm.

'Not in anything I do, of course. But in how I look at things.'

'And everyone sees things differently,' said Garrad.

'But not as differently as colour TV sees them,' said the

79

other with a laugh. Garrad said nothing. He pretended
to look around him at the world. He didn't tell this couple
that he'd come to like the blue-tinged eggs, the etherialized
pink of TV flesh. He'd had half a mind to tell them, if only
they had been more sympathetic, that these days he found
the world painfully hard-edged, almost too real, too steadily
bright for comfort.

'And anyway,' the husband was saying. 'Do I *want* it
all in colour? Why not save something I can discover for
myself.'

'Such as ...?' his wife asked.

'Well, let's say the foothills of the Himalayas.'

'You've left that pretty late,' she said. 'I don't think
you're going to make it. And anyway I'm not worrying
about what *you* might or might not discover. What about
all the invalids who can't get around at all? Don't you
want them to get the benefit of seeing the world in colour?'

'Listen! That's the first time she's ever mentioned
invalids and TV. It's all a ruse to make me sound selfish.
And talking of invalids, I may say it's the operations she'll
go for first if ever we get the colour. I mean the open heart
and the bisected brain are going to look quite something,
don't you think?' They moved swiftly on their way towards
home.

Garrad remained looking around him for a while, then
wandered slowly back along the way he'd come. The colour
was beginning to go out of the streets and into the sky.
Alleys, archways, back-courts were all a deeper grey, but
the upper air was glowing. The open heart. He repeated
it to himself. Now there was a phrase—a suggestive phrase
if ever there was one. It had a life apart from the operating
table. And there were some more prone to speak of hearts
than others. Open hearts or broken hearts, warm hearts

or cold ones—such words were easy for some people. But not to him. He never mentioned this heart to anyone, not even to himself. Yet it was real all right. In the world where he longed to put his hand on all real things—heart still had meaning. He slowed down. His heart was beating steadily as it had done for the last sixty years, as it would do for the next—how many more? 'Well, I'm not so crazy about a long life,' he had murmured out loud. In the doorway of his shop, near closing-time, James Byers heard him, heard the murmur 'not so crazy', and murmured very softly in reply:

'Now who would ever call *you* crazy, Mr Garrad?'

Garrad stopped abruptly, turned to the doorway and saw the spread of the evening newspaper, dark with disaster, and above it Byers' impassive face with its spectacled, secretive eyes watching him. The shop had no need of billboards. Here, morning and evening in the doorway Byers spread and read the paper. Passers-by read snippets hungrily and went in for more.

'I said I'm not all that crazy about a long life,' said Garrad. 'Look at old Peterson now, fumigated and isolated in that high-class nursing-home. I dread what I'll become. In his own home, my father—if he's anything to go by—was such a nuisance to himself and everyone else from his eighty-eighth to his ninety-first, poor man, that his funeral went like a regular jamboree. The surprise was there was no cavorting and singing.'

'You might be interested in a longer life when you come to it.'

'I doubt that. Ask me if you're still around.'

'I'll do that. This isn't your usual time for walking, Garrad—on a Wednesday evening.'

'It's not. I'm running from a sort of hole in our house.'

'A plumbing job?'

'No, not plumbing.'

'Hole? If my sister heard it she'd think of mice before you could say "tail". Even rats. There are rats behind those stinking old station sheds and plenty of them.'

'The hole I'm thinking of is a squared off bit of empty space.'

'Ah ... so we're on the metaphysical plane, are we?'

'Maybe. Our colour's gone. The box is away.'

'And you with it. Are you destroyed?'

'No, but it makes you think.'

Byers folded his paper impatiently and held it together in one hand while he adjusted his glasses the better to see a clock some blocks further up the street. He was a reader. In the evenings, after listening for a certain self-specified time to the complaints of customers who rang him about his paperboys, he would go off to the library—the phone still buzzing behind him. Once there, he would go through a further set of papers and magazines and return near closing-time with a pile of books under his arm. Garrad sensed the impatience of this man, but he went doggedly on: 'It makes you wonder about what's real and what isn't. Or whether it's all one. A TV tree and one outside the window, for instance. Would it matter if you never saw the outside one again? Or is it better?'

'So we're on morals now,' said Byers. 'Good, bad and better has nothing to do with it.'

'Maybe not. But I want to make sure I *feel* the difference between them.'

'Pleasure's the only thing that matters. The thing that gives you most—that's the one to go for.' There was a silence. Byers held his paper up again and they were joined by an old woman who scanned the headlines for a moment, decided against the full version, and shuffled off.

'Women have this way of skimming the cream off everything,' said Byers. 'It seems to satisfy them and at the same time they get it for nothing. But you were saying ...?'

'Real and unreal. One day at lunchtime, a while back, coming out of a restaurant I bent down to a table near the door and tried to smell a vase of those small, red artificial roses. Oh, very real they were! As I sniffed several people sitting near saw me, and guffawed.'

'But did you get no pleasure?'

'None. It was a very unpleasant sensation. What next? Maybe next time I'll be asking the way of a scarecrow. I was afraid it would grow on me—mixing up real and unreal. I didn't feel one hundred per cent human.'

'Well who is? Don't worry. And concentrate on pleasure.'

Garrad stared at him, at his melancholy mouth, downturned, as though by the continual drag of the dark headlines he held beneath his chin. 'So you've no colour,' Byers said suddenly as Garrad was moving quietly away. 'Better try walking westwards.'

In the west it was smouldering up into a sunset, not yet in full blaze. There was already a glow around him, but Garrad's thoughts were grey. He felt some loneliness walking back by himself in the pale pink. Even his own talk of real and unreal had unnerved him a bit. He'd been lucky to meet a few people, but he needed more than that. He was turning in now to a long street of identical houses whose front-room windows were so close to the pavement you could have almost touched the glass by stretching over one strip of grass, narrow as a doormat. The difference between one place and the next lay mainly in these green doormats—some were well-groomed and plushy, others

83

were threadbare or dotted with daisies. Now the pink light, growing deeper, illumined housefronts, stained smooth doorsteps and glinted overhead from a thick bristling of aerials. Most curtains were still not drawn and he had a full view into front rooms. He went more slowly. Most people had already switched on. In some rooms there were families, in others single persons—all bathed in a mixture of pink, and ghostly TV light. At one house the box flickered over an empty room. Garrad stood staring at a fisherman until a woman appeared in the doorway, stood watching the fisherman for a time, and went out again. Again she came back, switched from fisherman to skyscrapers to a shampooed head and back to the fisherman. She went out again and Garrad moved on. The fisherman was now on most screens and on one in four he was in colour. It made a fine colour-picture. The fisherman was knee-deep in a river on a summer evening and it was an evening which seemed to keep step with the actual evening outside. The river was flowing red just as the pavement where Garrad walked was beginning to glow. He went more and more slowly. Where groups sat he saw only profiles and backs of heads and at one or two windows heard snatches of screen commentary. Here whole families were sitting, spellbound or bound by boredom. He had the feeling that if he stepped over and tapped at these windows not a head would turn. If a head *did* turn and he beckoned —who would exert the strongest pull? He with his fires behind him or the fisherman with his? He felt unfairly matched for he was now tired. He imagined he made a rather poor picture compared with the rapt river-man. Not even switched on. To all intents and purposes, though with the red behind, an invisible man.

Garrad was three-quarters down this long street when

he met his match. A dozen houses or so from the end he turned his head towards one wide window and saw—himself. He was set up like all the rest of them, handsomely framed and mounted—the same for size, the same for clarity. His background glowed out stronger and redder even than the fisherman's. He was looking into a mirror which stood squarely in that place where in all other rooms he had looked for the TV set. It was an old-fashioned mirror set up on a stand, like a picture on a short easel, and placed on a side-table well away from the wall. The room itself was identical to all the other rooms of the street. Yet in atmosphere it was different. It lacked the sealed-off, all absorbed look of the others. There was no spellbinder here—only two young women who, backs to the window, were bending over the end of a long table. It wasn't easy to see what they were doing. They might be wrapping and tying a dumpy parcel from the look of it, or pressing and persuading a yeasty lump of dough. They stood aside for a moment and he saw a baby being zipped into a night-sack. Its head rolled on the tabletop. Its furious feet made the corners of the bag squirm like a flame-curled envelope. Garrad watched the performance. For more than half the street he'd been an invisible screen-watcher, familiar only with the backs of heads. But now one of the women, catching sight of his head in the mirror, twisted round to face him. This double look fascinated Garrad. At one blow he was twice hailed, twice identified as a living man. Now the other woman had turned. As though aware of some oddness in their background, lacking a TV, they did more than turn their heads. They seemed amused at the man gaping in at them. One of them swung the baby in its bag up off the table and both came to the window and pushed it wider open. Garrad leaned on the gate. The baby was placed on the window-ledge, its white woollen bag absorbing sunset like a sponge.

'Talk about fire!' exclaimed the young mother leaning out. 'That sky is quite something!'

'The best I've seen for years,' Garrad replied.

'He's never seen one yet,' she said, hitching the baby further up. 'It's his first, I believe. This *is* his first.' Garrad felt that only with reluctance had the baby let his fury subside. At any moment it might burst again. Meanwhile it continued to stare out.

'It's not the sky that interests him,' said the other, who was obviously a sister. 'I don't believe he'd so much as blink if the sky turned suddenly green or black or whatever. *People* interest him.'

'He loves *colour*. And I believe he even looks at distance,' said the mother. Stern and impassive, the baby hung between them while they bickered gently behind his back. There was some jealousy around. Even Garrad felt jealous for himself. He had alerted them to colour. He *was* colour. His shoulders and back were saturated with it, his hair pronged with pink. Between their shoulders he got a glimpse of himself in the mirror with great streaks of fire behind his head.

'Yes, it was seeing you in *that*,' said the sister following his glance. 'If you hadn't stopped just where you are we wouldn't have noticed until too late. It's past its best already, isn't it?' Garrad was appeased. He was about to move on when there was a flash of lightning and some moments later a distant rumble of thunder.

'Oh I knew that was coming!' said the girl holding the baby. There was another flash behind Garrad's left shoulder followed directly by a much louder boom. The women at the window were now staring at him transfixed.

He was something now all right with his flaming sky and lightning springing between his shoulders. For a moment all three were satisfied to stare—the women at the sudden drama outside, the man at the scene indoors. But the baby, peeved by the momentary withdrawal of attention, began to girn and twist in its bag.

'You'll excuse us if we shut the window now,' said its mother. 'But thanks—thanks for drawing our attention ...'

Garrad waved. He saw his own hand move in their mirror and again got the double response, as they faced him and as they turned inwards and saw his image. He moved away, past more family groups, past couples and single viewers. The fisherman had long ago packed up and a dozen soldiers were galloping with spears poised through a narrow gorge between mountains. Thunder was rumbling very far off. Garrad walked slowly though he was still a long way from his own part of the town. The fiery sky was already half extinguished, yet for a short time the colour down in the streets seemed deeper than ever, as if trapped and richly mixed with dark stone or floating through the dust and soot in the air. By the time Garrad reached his district the whole upper sky had faded to a yellow-green, but here and there between the distant cranes and spires on the town's horizon there were still some streaks of orange light. He turned another corner, walked up a long street of empty offices and shops and out into the part where the double villas and careful gardens began. He was near home. A few steps further and he was looking into his own front room. The place was lit but deserted and the square of emptiness where the TV had stood seemed more conspicuous than ever. Yet as soon as he was in the door he knew the heavy atmosphere had fractionally lifted. A moment later his wife came through from the back of the house.

'The colour's coming back!' she said.

'It's what?'

'They phoned soon after you left. And there's not all that much wrong. We'll have the colour back first thing tomorrow.'

'Well, thank God for that.' His gratitude for the returning colour-box sounded thin to his own ears. The very flatness of his tone gave the lie to it. Yet when it did come tomorrow wouldn't he welcome colour back with open arms? He didn't doubt it. At this moment, however, he was loaded with the stuff himself. The new substance. The real thing. His clothes were soaked in it to the skin. The whole gamut of reds had penetrated to his bone marrow and was now thickening his blood. But he was not, as far as he could see, radiating any of this spectacular colour himself. His wife looked blank. The hall was dim and getting dimmer. On the right hung a large mirror and on the opposite side a smaller one reflecting into infinity a square of biscuit-toned wall. Between these Garrad moved forward carefully but stopped at the foot of the stairs. His wife was watching him closely.

'What are you thinking about?' she said.

'Colour, of course.'

'Are you thinking about the missing colour?'

'No, just colour.'

'*Not* the missing colour?'

'No. Colour.'

'What, to be exact?'

'The usual. Starting with that odd tree that sticks out into the road. Never noticed before but it's got half its bark peeled off. Every boy that passes tears a strip. It's dead

88

white on the pavement side, black on the other. It's a cartoon tree now.'

'Black and white? Are you still talking about colour?'

'I went past the market. Rails and rails of red, blue and yellow dresses. Who buys them?'

'What's so *new*?'

'Nothing. I went as far as the school with the glass. There's actually a palm-tree in the corridor. Imagine it! There'll not be much stripped off *that* one. And back again. The stalls were packing up. People fingering huge piles of bashed plums and split tomatoes.' He paused.

'What else?'

Garrad had his foot on the stairs. 'The sky.' He drew his breath with a slight hiss. 'There's still a patch.'

'A patch?'

'Of red. Of pink now. You might still see something from the back room. One patch left, and getting smaller every minute.' He started to go up. His wife who had been staring at him as though expecting the knobs of his backbone to light up, now stood reluctantly pondering the pale pink patch, her foot on the bottom stair. Slowly she went up after him.

Waiting for the Sun

'I don't know whether you've seen this one before,' Mr
Shering would say, passing the photo round a company
at his fireside. 'A fellow at my hotel took that—never seen
the man in my life. He bobbed up in front of me one day
—and that was it! Not so much as "by your leave".' Walking across to the lamp he would study another one for a
long time, murmuring to himself: 'I haven't an idea where
this one was taken. Wait a minute though. Wasn't I just
stepping off the boat at Marseilles? It must have been the
mother of that child who took such a fancy to me for some
unknown reason. And here's another. Believe it or not,
this time I simply haven't a clue. As likely as not some
complete stranger took it when I wasn't looking. These
things happen to me!' But his sideways glance as he
passed between two handsome mirrors which hung on
opposite walls clearly showed that he saw every reason why
such things should happen to him. In these glasses he was
reflected, diminished but shining, within an infinite number of gilded frames—a tall, heavily-built man in his six-
ties who carried himself as though he had, in the past, held
his chin up over a series of stiff collars and was now keeping it that way, no longer supported by the formal neck-
wear but simply by the memory of these people who had
once turned to stare at him as he went by and wondered

who he was. An actor, a visiting conductor, some distinguished man of letters? Once he had kept them guessing. Nowadays he thrived only on a few upturned faces staring at him from his own fireside, or the brief turning of heads as he laboriously boarded the trains and buses of out-of-the-way towns. He had to make the most of these rarer and rarer occasions when he believed himself recognized for what he was.

This need was greater now. All the same, he was hard put to know what he was himself. He occasionally referred to his 'full life', but somehow he had missed doing anything which gave him the right to display a label or put out a sign. Moreover, since he was a young man there had grown up a much greater demand for exact self-description and the clear listing of virtues and vices in black and white. Confident 'yes' or 'no' answers to quick-firing questions were now expected as a matter of course. In the days when he had money it had been different. It was enough then to set out a tray of ornaments before his visitors and to keep a silk polishing cloth and a magnifying glass at hand for studying details and inscriptions. In no time he would find himself described by at least one of the company as an antiquarian. He had only to unhook one or two dark brown oil paintings from the walls and study them under the light, or thumb reverently through a worn leather-bound book—and he was unlucky if two or three did not refer to him as a connoisseur of painting or collector of rare books. It was a matter of picking the right company and keeping them at a certain distance so that there could be no question of disillusionment on either side. He respected other people's feelings and was extremely tender with his own. He deplored the growing tendency to probe and question. Born sceptics were nothing more or less than bores to his way of thinking, and he had a particular dislike for those who, in season and out, were avid for the truth. He looked on them as selfish people, greedy for a special form of nourishment which had always been hard to procure, and was in any case a luxury which he himself had been able to do without for years on end.

Some loss in income made a difference to his way of living for a time. His health was affected, but only enough to keep him mooning about the convalescent wings of nursing-homes and from there to the back gardens and spare bedrooms of various acquaintances during the summer. When after a few years he took up his interests again, he discovered the world was changing out of all recognition. Speed and absolute efficiency were demanded, even for the forming of relationships. On every side there was a gathering in of facts and information, while the tools and mechanical devices for detecting flaws in machines and human beings were working overtime. He suspected that they were contained, when not in use, in the shiny plastic bags and steel-hinged cases which were everywhere being carried about in place of the crushable, bulging ones he had known.

He began to move about in a world of his own, politely ignoring the people who asked him what he did, staring intently over the heads of those who tried to tell him what they did themselves. Long ago he had discovered it was not necessary to listen to every word spoken. Only a few words were needed in order to place the speaker. The rest had been a matter of patience—unending, unquestioning patience. But now, like it or not, he was moving into the sink-or-swim era of experts. Mr Shering realized he would sink without trace unless he found a new and effortless way to assert himself.

It was the necessity to combine being somebody with doing nothing which led him to his new interest. In no time it amounted to an obsession. In place of the prints and paintings and glittering trays of little knick-knacks, fat albums of photos began to pile up on top of his bookcase. When his finances improved and he began to move about again and see the world the interest came into full force. The time came when he could hand round photos dating back over years and point out the details which had a topical interest at the time.

'This was that town where there was all the rumpus—nine years ago—over the leading councillor. If you look closely I think you might just see his name chalked up in white on that wall there. The abuse was in red underneath —bigger letters in fact, but you'd have to have good eyes to see it. It's the red against the dark wall does it. And here's one in Sicily. It's supposed to be a photo of the volcano of course, but here's the tail-end of a bus come in the way. Incidentally that same bus was in the news a day or two later—overturned into a ravine with a load of tourists. It's rather a horrid photo, I'm afraid—the more so when you remember the volcano started erupting six months or so later!'

People looking through these photos were more surprised, however, to see their extraordinary variety. There were all types here from small, blurred, amateur snaps to the studies whose light and clarity approached professional standard. Sometimes at first glance they made the mistake of imagining that Shering was himself the photographer. Nothing could be further from the truth and their mistake was quickly corrected on a closer inspection. While Mr Shering was pointing out the palm-trees, flags, ruins and mountains which marked his travels, his

93

guests were studying the figure, dignified and solitary, standing sometimes in the middle distance but more often in the foreground of each photo. Though his appearance in these pictures changed over the years, though his clothes varied with the summer or winter backgrounds against which he stood—like those animals whose brown coats turn white against the snow—he was always easy to spot. Shering never had to point himself out. He simply referred to the many friends he made as he went about, travellers like himself who'd taken him up on the spot as though they'd known him all their lives. He was lucky, he supposed, to have met the people who took him as they found him.

But the real reason was that though the world had changed he'd no intention of being left out of the picture. The desire to be photographed had grown from the need to be in contact again with persons who could admire him from a distance. This distance, lengthening with each disillusionment, gradually became the space between himself and the person with a camera. There was a fascination about such a contact. It was intimate yet impersonal. It was with people who, except for one sunlit encounter, would remain strangers to him for the rest of his life.

It was not others who took him as they found him. It was he who found and captured all those with cameras in their hands, recognizing them even from a great distance by their surroundings and gestures, as a birdwatcher spots his special birds. He would then come running heavily down some cliff path or down the worn steps of a cathedral, breathlessly descending to the beach or crowded square where someone was balancing their black box against a rock or the rim of a fountain. 'Hullo there!' he would shout while still some distance off. 'Wait a minute! Have you got that quite right? You're going to spoil a magnificent

94

picture if you're not careful. Hold on. I'll be right with you!'

Occasionally he made mistakes in the people he approached. Any other man might have been struck to the ground by the looks certain photographers directed towards him as he came waving and running. He had withstood some terrible abuse in his time. But such incidents were rare. In any case the skin which appeared to be drawn so finely over Shering's well-cut features was surprisingly thick. And years of practice had enabled him to spot the amateur almost without fail. When this happened it was no time till he'd struck up a conversation with someone behind an out-of-date camera, not long either before he was standing, his head turned away, his profile white as marble against some dingy ruin or black as basalt against a sun-whitened archway—waiting for the click which would release him from a casual, dreaming posture. 'Is that how you want me? Tell me when you've got it,' he would murmur, scarcely opening his lips or lowering his eyelids. 'Well, if you can really be bothered,' he would say in parting, drawing out a visiting card with his home address. 'It would be a memento of a very happy meeting, of a most interesting talk.' It was in this way that his collection of photos grew.

In great cities the poses Shering took up were sculpturesque. His look could be stern and sorrowful like the expression on statues in public squares. Occasionally his face, which showed the mildness of a sheltered life, could take on the look of a man of violent action—an expression he'd caught sight of on some nearby helmeted figure mounted on a bronze war-horse. On the other hand photos taken in the country showed him as natural and pliable as his backgrounds. He was snapped leaning on gates or bend-

95

ing down to study a flower in the grass—always looking up at the right moment to flash a smile. He had no attractive wife to steal the picture, no restless children to smudge the effect in the foreground. He was suspicious of all tricks in photography—gadgets which made a raindrop on a cabbage leaf bulge like a crown jewel. People who used these devices tended to be more complicated than the others and might show less patience for taking straightforward pictures of himself. In spite of everything he maintained he had more friends all over the world than he could ever keep up with. The friends he spoke of were simply those people with whom he had sat and waited for the sun.

The hours he had sat waiting for the sun took up the greater part of Mr Shering's waking life. He had sat waiting with people amongst ruins, on the edge of piers, on mountains, in boats and in buses. Infinitely adaptable, he could wait calmly with a solitary and tongue-tied tourist winding the first reel into his camera as with the seasoned traveller already halfway round the world. Long habits of posing had given him an expression of concentration which never wavered, whether he was listening to the endless comparisons of hotel bedrooms or to the peculiar history of certain engraved stones set in a nearby arch. He was not attending. The brightening gleam in his eyes was not evidence of the climax to a thrilling tale but of the long-awaited appearance of the sun at the edge of a bank of black cloud.

It was the sun which held all things together in Mr Shering's disconnected life. His casual encounters were made only in its light, and faded when the light faded. Under heavy skies he lived from hour to hour, dulled and diminished in his own eyes, making few contacts, seeing and hearing little of what was going on around him. But he knew when the sun rose and when it set on every day of the year. Elusive as its shining was, the sun was the only dependable in a monstrously unreliable life.

One fine morning in summer, Shering, who was coming to the end of a fortnight's holiday near the south-west coast, decided that for his final outing he would climb as high as he could to get a last view of the sea and the surrounding country. The small hotel where he had been staying had become inexplicably crowded the evening before, and he'd decided to move on as soon as possible. Crowds were not for him. He needed a great deal of time and space for himself and he had resented this inrush of young men and women who overnight had transformed the quiet hotel into a place as busy and noisy as a city office. The irritation vanished, however, as soon as he'd left the village and taken the path which led up through a group of young birch trees onto the slope above. This was the only hill in the district and it counted as high. But the climb was easy. The air was clear. As he went up, the blue spaces of the sky widened out and the mist rolled off the fields until at last he was able to look down at the sea sparkling in full sunshine below. He took the last part of the climb slowly, scarcely looking up till he reached the boulders which marked the top. When he did raise his head and stop for breath he saw a young man already seated there. Shering marked with approval the camera slung on his shoulder. But he also saw as he came closer that the man belonged to the party which had arrived at the hotel the evening before.

Shering remembered him all too clearly—this business-like fellow packed with information of one kind or another who'd made it perfectly plain to the rest of the company,

97

as he spread out maps and plans and diagrams, that he and his friends were not on holiday like the rest of them, but were involved in some project of the utmost interest to the entire world. Shering had got well out of earshot long before the nature of this research could be explained. Being on perpetual holiday himself, he had an instinctive suspicion of people who discussed work enthusiastically in public and a particular dislike of those who, groaning at the swift passing of time, insisted on counting up the few days of freedom left to them. Freedom lay heavily on Shering from one year's end to the next—limitless and all-enveloping. Long ago the word had lost its meaning. When he heard it discussed he felt as much resentment as if words from an unknown language had been suddenly thrust into the conversation. It had seemed to him possible, as he watched the earnest young men and women, that at any minute there might burst on his ears the question of time wasted and made up, a discussion of extra efforts to be made, of timetables, calendars and the hour-by-hour recording of important events. He had gone early to bed.

The young man on top of the hill, however, showed no particular emotion on seeing Shering. His face was thin and stern and his dark eyes stared confidently out from behind horn-rimmed spectacles. To the older man who was climbing laboriously up towards him he gave the impression, even though slight and rigid in build, that at this moment he owned the hill, the sky, the sea, and the whole surrounding countryside. He was absolute master of the situation, whatever it was, and this time Shering himself had not an inkling how the land lay. The young man gave no clue and threw out no communication line. But Shering, secretive himself, knew he was bursting with some purpose of his own. He was not here for the view. Not a muscle of his body was relaxed.

'We are far too early of course,' he remarked as Shering came up, and he gave a short laugh as though scorning himself, 'but I prefer to take up my position before the others arrive.' He seemed relieved that the necessity of speech was over and done with. He turned away at once and examined the sea with exaggerated curiosity. Shering sat down on the smoothest boulder and looked around him.

'It *is* early.' He spoke politely to the rigid shoulders. 'But not an unnatural time for me to be out and about, I can assure you. I think it's safe to say there won't be anyone else around for some time—unless of course you're expecting friends.'

The young man turned his head slightly to one side, but said nothing. It now became clear that the set of his face was due to extreme nervousness. He sat straight, his arms tightly folded across his chest as though rigidly controlling himself. Shering, who prided himself on putting all kinds of people at their ease, felt instinctively that this would be as hard a case as he had yet tackled.

'I somehow imagine—I may be quite out—I imagine from certain things you said last night that you are a teacher,' he began in the hesitating voice which overlaid an inexhaustible persistence.

'Science,' the young man muttered through his teeth.

'A teacher of Science,' said Shering with an edge of disapproval to his voice. 'Then in many ways I think I envy you. To be able to convey something of the mystery ... something of the miracle ...' But the young man was staring at the sky where a long strip of cloud was drifting across the sun. His face grew more than ever pinched and severe, and when at last the sun was completely covered he

99

jumped to his feet with a groan. Shering saw what he could only describe as a tearing of hair, and he was amazed. Nothing in his opinion could account for such emotion, unless the relation between cloud and camera. But though he had stood by and watched the disappointment of hundreds of photographers—never had he witnessed a disappointment like this. By this time he also was on his feet and now stood with folded arms, his head flung back watching the sky. He had seen all this before. A whole continent of cloud might move across to blot out the sun. He could be patient.

'If I'm not mistaken it will all pass over in about twenty minutes or so,' he said quietly. 'You'll have your picture, if that's what's worrying you. Indeed, if I'm any judge of cameras, that one there will take a very fine picture in just this light.' But as he spoke these words he knew they were worse than useless—he even judged them downright dangerous. For the young man had turned abruptly. Shering found himself looking into a pair of glaring eyes, eyebrows raised in outrage above the hornrims. It was a fanatic's face. At any minute he could be expected to raise his fists in the air and curse Shering for ever having set foot on the same hill as himself.

'I have as much right ...' began Shering, taking a step back and glancing behind as he did so. But what he saw below him cut short all stating of rights.

A great crowd of people were slowly making their way up onto this hill where, in the last fortnight, not a soul had set foot. They came from all sides—men, women and children, winding their way purposefully along the grassy paths at the foot and looking up now and then with an air of expectancy towards the top where the two men stood. Further out in the lanes below Shering saw that cars were drawing up. Beyond that again and for as far as he could see, cars, vans and caravans were coming in, one behind the other, all along the criss-crossed roads of the surrounding district. Twisting through them and wobbling behind were long, glittering lines of bicycles, with the odd motorbike coming up, jolting and bursting, from the rear. Every now and then those on foot who'd been pressed back into the hedges by passing traffic, widened out again in pairs or groups across the road and were passed in their turn by some solitary figure with a knapsack who had been plodding along since early morning. There was a continual movement going on—a knotting, a fanning out, a stepping back and forward. But there was no chaos on the roads. A single purpose drove them forward towards the foot of the hill where the first arrivals were climbing out of their cars and had started to move up behind the rest onto the lower slopes. In a few minutes solid ranks of people, close enough to hide the green, were climbing from all sides over rocks and through bushes, coming on with the silent determination of an army on the move. There was something strange to Shering in that determination. Were they converging on *him*? In one panic second his innocent life flashed by. For what crime was he to be punished on the hill? To placate what gods?

The panic passed. Looking closer he could make out specific groups among the crowd. Small family parties emerged with rugs and raincoats over their arms. Some carried thermos flasks, lemonade bottles and wads of sandwiches in brown paper. Shades of navy blue marked the circles of pupils from surrounding schools, accompanied by their teachers. Here and there official uniforms stood out. A driver and his conductor were coming up with a bus load of passengers. A couple of off-duty policewomen were going along with them, while down at the foot five nuns were paying off a taxi, chattering excitedly, their black habits blowing behind them as they turned to climb. Most prominent amongst the crowd was the large group of young men recognized by Shering as the group who had arrived at the hotel the evening before. It was at once clear to him that they, along with his companion in the hornrims, were the natural leaders of this gathering. They did not spread themselves like the others and their heavy, angular equipment had nothing to do with picnics. They were serious if not actually grim as they climbed up silently together to join the young man at the top.

Most of the crowd had now gathered on the highest part of the hill and soon the grass was patched with raincoats where the families were sitting down, already surreptitiously unscrewing thermos flasks. But there was something different here from the usual picnicking crowd. These people were focused outwards. It was more than a normal interest in the view. Their eyes remained mesmerically fixed even while they poured the tea and put their hands in and out of paper bags. Shering saw a few miss their mark and more than one stream of tea flowed down the side of a mug into the grass. Meanwhile those solitary persons who had come up to roam restlessly about on their own, now met and passed one another without a glance, only dropping their eyes from the distance once in a while to stare at watches.

Surrounded as he was on all sides, Shering felt increasingly ill at case, like the solitary unbeliever in a crowd of visionaries. If he was conspicuous it was because he lacked the expectancy which marked all other faces, and feeling safer unobserved, he sat down cautiously on the ground. All the signs now persuaded him that he was part of a great open-air organization—a political or religious sect grown strong and drawing followers from a vast area. At any moment an orator would spring to his feet. There would be answering shouts and chants and a raising of banners with secret slogans. Shering had watched such things before, but always from a distance. His spirits sank. It was too late to make his escape. There was now an unmistakable rounding-up going on. Teachers were gathering in the pupils who had strayed too far and here and there a parent was running after a child who'd broken away to other family groups. The bus driver had placed himself in front of his passengers in order to count them, his lips moving, his eyes going from face to face. The nuns stood quietly together, their tilted, white-bound brows towards the sky, arms on their skirts. While all around the groups drew closer and closer together, a hush had gradually fallen on the crowd. Shering noticed it first in the nearby families who had stopped talking and seemed to be taking care to fold up their paper with as little sound as possible. Nobody hurried. There was almost stealth in the movement about him and those who had got to their feet did it as though fearful of disturbing the earth they stood on. More and more people were staring at their watches and with an intentness uncanny to Mr Shering to whom time meant nothing. And now the silence which had deepened with every second was broken suddenly by a rustling whisper which swept over the crowd as they bent towards one another like reeds over which an unnatural wind had passed. Shering listened intently to the curious sound which came again and again from those nearest him. 'The sun!' It was this word he managed to sift from all the rest. It grew steadily in volume until it seemed his own secret sun obsession was being declaimed from all sides.

'So that's it,' he said to calm himself, unaware that he was whispering like the rest. 'Well, what of it?' He saw only a bright, mottled sky with one darker strip of cloud hiding the sun. He saw nothing strange. It was the same sky he had always stared at, the same cloud hiding the longed-for sun.

'Are you waiting for the sun to come out?' he said, throwing his words with enormous effort into a silence. No one answered, but several faces turned momentarily in his direction—shocked faces staring at a blasphemer. Swiftly they turned away again towards the sky.

Shering had gradually become aware that for the last few minutes a peculiar gloom had been falling through the air. He noticed it first upon his blanching hands. Then he saw the grass. It had faded as though a sudden blight had eaten up its green. Now sea and sky turned grey. If a great storm was impending it was not from the few clouds overhead—but rather from some black cloud rolling up to cover the whole earth. Shering's only thought was for shelter. But there was no shelter for him on the hill. He saw the sky change to the north and the ground, as far as the eye could see, turned grey as though sprinkled with ash. All over the hill, as the darkness deepened, there was a soft surge of movement as people inside the groups pressed closer and closer together while those on the outside swung in nearer to the others. Shering felt more than unsheltered. He was alone, unprepared for whatever disaster was about to break. For suddenly a single gust of cold wind passed over him, pricking up the hairs of his head. At the same instant, like a great net flung rifling into the sky, a flock of starlings went up behind him and took flight to the west. Shering raised both hands to his head and in the silence heard his own voice whisper: 'No! Not yet ...!' But this time the sun was no longer a partner in the game. He knew that in less than one minute he was to be witness to its eclipse.

The smoky yellow clouds covering the sun now turned dark red, changing as the darkness grew to a deep violet which Shering had never seen before, even in the most spectacular sunset. But the rest of the earth darkened and withered rapidly. The faces around him turned livid. Clothes, rocks, grass and blazing gorse bushes had faded to ghosts of themselves. Shering, like the survivor of some dying planet, was appalled to see a few stars shining in the clear patches of the sky. The last light faded and he covered his eyes. Stooping, his knees and shoulders limp as if even the red blood ran grey, he gave himself up to the darkest moment of the eclipse.

Half a minute later Shering found himself on the ground staring at the same landscape from which a heavy veil was being swiftly lifted. Colour was coming back over ground and sky with such speed that it seemed a thick membrane covering his eye had split to let in this astounding light. But in seconds this brilliance had faded again into the ordinary light of day. Over the whole hillside there was now an air of recovery and relief and from all sides there came a murmuring which grew gradually louder. Shouts and laughter broke out, and amongst certain groups violent discussions started up. The young men and women from the hotel were putting instruments back into their cases and tucking wedges of smoked glass into the pockets of haversacks between maps and charts. The eclipse had not been perfect. Shering could see the earnest young man standing apart from the others, still staring at the clouded sky, pale with disappointment. But the others had recovered from their frustration and were now rapidly making notes in small black exercise books. On all sides people were gathering themselves together, briskly brushing off the astounding along with the earth and grass from their coats.

Soon, over the round top of the hill, patches of green appeared again as groups started to move down the slopes —slowly at first, still dazed and chilled, then more quickly as they came further down where the grass was smooth. In a few minutes the whole hillside of people seemed to be taking part in a great race to see who could reach the level ground first. Where he sat Shering could feel the urgent beating of the earth under him. Flaps of coats and rugs brushed past his knees in a steady wind of movement, and once a swinging handbag tilted his hat over his eyes. Still he sat on, motionless, his eyes on the ground, feeling the racing current around him grow gradually less and less, until it was no more than a gentle fanning of the air as the last and slowest on the hill went past. Far down below, those who had reached the road were already starting up cars and pulling bicycles out of the hedges. The bus driver was in his seat patiently watching his passengers file in. The nuns, all folded and sober as birds after a flight, were waiting inside their taxi. The hikers were moving purposefully off down the lanes. Determined now to weld themselves to solid earth, nobody looked back and nobody looked up.

The last to leave the hill had been a group of schoolboys who'd waited for the lecture on what they had not, but might have seen. Their spirits were still high. As Shering had watched them race off he saw, halfway down, one of the group break away from the rest and come pounding up again towards the spot where he was sitting. As he came near the boy started to swing about in circles close to the ground. Now and then he pounced and raked the long grass with his toe. Nothing came of the search. His circles grew wider and dizzier, and he was already moving back downhill when there was a shout from above. 'I have it!' Shering was pointing to something red a few yards away in the grass. By the time he reached him the boy had fastened the red pen into his pocket and now flung himself, gasping, down beside Shering. 'A piece of luck!' he exclaimed when he could speak. 'I thought I'd never see it again!'

'It was lucky *I* saw it,' said Shering. He was not in the mood to speak of luck. Something about the boy's red face and the way he rolled himself exultantly on the ground reminded him that he himself had sat on the same spot, cold and motionless, for a very long time. His gloom and silence made itself felt.

'Why are you still here?' asked the boy, suddenly straightening up and staring at Shering with interest. 'Are you waiting for something more to happen? Because it won't. You've had it—probably for the rest of the century.'

Shering's eyes swept the horizon coldly. 'Nobody told me,' he said, speaking to the sky.

'We've known about it for months in our school,' said the boy. He took out a square of smoked glass, spat on it and polished it regretfully on his sleeve. 'A lot of use this was!' he said staring through it at the clouds. 'I could tell you all the eclipses for years back—totals and annulars. Of course you won't see a total till August 1999. Well honestly, I don't think you'll be around by that time, will you? But of course you might come in for a few lunars. By the way, did you ever hear of Bailey's Beads?'

'Never!' said Shering curtly. He took a quick look into the thick grass.

'Lots of people haven't,' said the boy with satisfaction. He was silent for some time, looking out over the countryside and relishing the widespread ignorance. Then he said: 'All the same, I wouldn't have missed that blackout. Did you know that one of the kids from Lower School nearly fainted? Our Maths man, Baker, laid him on his back and produced a bottle of whisky. That would have been a botch-up for a start. Even beginners First Aid know that. Anyway, you should have seen this infant's face! We thought he'd died. Imagine what a morning that would have been. Eclipse and corpse at one swoop! Well, he wasn't dead, but he was terribly sick afterwards. All the rest of us looked grey and white at the time. But do you know what colour *his* face was? It was blue—pale blue with purple shadows. Of course we'll be getting an essay on this, and I shall put in someone lying dead in an eclipse— and no one looking at him. If you saw it in a newspaper you wouldn't believe it, would you? You could be lying dead right here in the grass where we are now, and no one taking any notice—just staring at the sky.'

'It's too cold to sit,' said Shering getting up from the ground. 'As a matter of fact I only came up for fifteen minutes, and I've been over an hour. I don't care to catch a chill on the last day of my holiday.'

'But the sun's coming out,' said the boy. He drew a small flat camera from his gaberdine pocket. 'I've got one photo to get before I go.'

'What kind of thing do you want?' asked Shering, automatically taking his pose a few steps back.

'Well, as a matter of fact, I wouldn't mind a snap of myself,' said the boy. 'That is, if *you* don't mind. There's nothing else to take, is there? I'd like it right here on the spot where we saw it happen. It'll be unique. And maybe

I won't have the same interest even if it does happen again. I mean you hadn't been all that interested yourself in eclipses, had you? It goes to show you can't go on and on feeling excited about things forever.'

'And I thought boys of your age weren't all that excited about having their photos taken,' replied Shering sharply. 'Did you mean that *I* would take it?'

'Of course I would have asked one of the others,' said the boy. 'But they were all off like a shot. Anyway there's nothing in it. It's the simplest camera out. You simply press that—when I tell you. That's all there is to it. Wait a second!' He ran to a flat rock. 'What about this?' he called. 'Am I all right?' Shering didn't answer. He held the camera gingerly, bending his head only an inch or so as though over an unexploded bomb.

'Am I all right?' came the shout again. 'Can you see me?'

'Of course I can see you!' Shering lifted his head and glared before him. The boy was sitting on the rock with his knees drawn up, his hands clasped around them, and on his face the serious obliquely-focused look of one born to be photographed. Shering experienced a sudden crippling spasm of jealousy.

'I'll send you a copy if it comes out!' called the boy. 'Press now!' His lips, Shering noted, scarcely moved.

'What are we waiting for?' called the boy again. 'The light's all right, isn't it. Have you got the sun behind you?'

Shering turned and stared in the direction of the sun. It was there where it should be, shining serenely over a quiet hillside. Except for the flattened squares of grass and a few empty paper bags there was no sign that anything unusual had taken place. But the face which Shering turned to the sun was utterly changed. It was no longer that of a trusting man, but rather of someone who can now believe anything of his accomplice—even that day might become night or night day before he can turn his head.

Among the photos which Shering showed to visitors there appeared, from time to time, one on which he made little or no comment. At first sight it was naturally supposed to be a rather dim photo of Shering himself, taken in his schoolboy days. He was, after all, there in every other photo they had seen, and there was even something reminiscent of him in this small figure who sat with averted profile and firmly posed hands and feet. But Shering was quick to correct the mistake. 'This—of the schoolboy— is the one I took myself,' he would say in a voice more restrained than usual, and in the silence which followed he would add in a low tone, still more sternly controlled: '... The sun disappeared for a time.' Nothing more was said, and no question ever asked, though during the swift appearance and disappearance of this photo it occasionally occurred to imaginative visitors that the man might even be hiding the fact that he had a son. But Shering, putting it back carefully into the middle of a pack of photos like a man hiding an unlucky card, gave them to understand that this was one snapshot on which, dim as it was, he had no intention of throwing any further light.

Just Answer Yes or No

'But I filled up something like this a few weeks ago!' said the old woman in the red cap, striking out the M of the M/F question with a bold dash of her pen. 'They should know I'm still female. They ought to know that! I don't mind them wondering if it's the same country, the same town or the same job. They've a right to ask if it's the same husband, same sister-in-law, the same dog, mouse, cat or canary, the same toothache, bellyache or backache. But by this time they should know I'm female. I look female, don't I?' The woman was rather fat and she sat with the round cap pulled down over her ears, leaning her big, woollen bust against the top of the café table while she filled up the form. She looked soft but tough. The form was long and as she filled it up it moved, guided by her fingers, across the table, millimetre by millimetre, between cups and saucers and round the central breadplate till it was almost at the other side. A married couple who sat at the same table had been watching silently, but now the man leaned forward.

'That's all very well,' he said, 'but these people can't take any chances. Everything changes, as you say. People change their age year by year of course. They change their address and sometimes their names. Isn't it common knowledge they can even change their sex? Somebody's got to keep check or things could get wildly out of hand in no time. You've got to look at it that way.'

'Let her look at it any way she wants,' said his wife. 'The way I'm looking I can see it's rather a pretty form. It's in three parts so far—pink, white and green, but I can see there's lots more to come and probably other colours into the bargain. I like the way they get these things up now-adays. There's some style to them.' The old woman worked in silence for some time, then paused and looked back over what she'd done.

'Can I help you with that?' asked the man leaning across again. 'I mean,' he added quickly as she looked up, 'have you given all the Particulars they want? General Particulars?'

'I've finished that bit,' she said. 'I'm starting Section Two.'

'That's fine then. Just go on as you've been doing.'

'I've left a few empty spaces. But I suppose I can go back to them later.'

'Of course,' said the man. 'Get on with the next bit.'

The old woman was now putting crosses in the spaces left for them. As she bent her head and her fingers moved it was easier to imagine her sticking a heavy needle in and out of a piece of tough cloth, or pinching an edging of dough round the rim of a dish. Her fingers were short and strong. The paper seemed too smooth for her. There was a snaky slickness about it which was not agreeable, though it made the job easier if it had to be done. The woman went on.

'Anyway, that looks a nicer section you're on now,' said the man's wife leaning sideways to watch her.

'How—"nicer"?' said the man.

'Well, it's going to be made up of little X's when she's done.'

'That's right,' said the old woman pointing to the heading: PUT AN X WHERE APPLICABLE. 'It's easier than Section One. You've not got to think.'

'Yes,' said the wife again. 'It's going to be rather attractive when it's all filled up. It's the pattern. It looks like columns of kisses.' Her husband made a contemptuous sound and snapped his fingers above the table between them.

'I know what I'm talking about,' said his wife. 'This way it *is* prettier. The Particulars didn't make much of a pattern. Too haphazard. This looks consistent and after all that's what design is. Consistent.' The three of them were silent for some time—the couple watching and the old woman criss-crossing down the form.

'Wait a minute though,' said the man suddenly, leaning over. 'What have you been doing?' The old woman gave a groan and stopped. 'What now?' she said.

'There's something wrong here,' said the man. 'They can't want solid columns of crosses. Obviously they want a break somewhere, or what's the point of it?'

'I'm not to go over it,' said the old woman grimly. 'Right or wrong, that bit's to stay.'

'Well make a break in it then. Start leaving blanks here and there—say every five or so. They've got to count them too. Blanks are important. You can't fool them. They want the blanks, believe me, as much or *more* than the crosses!'

'My husband's quite right,' said his wife. 'And that's the peculiar thing about official forms. If you try to please you're going to make them mad. I think the kindest thing is to give them a real mixture of stuff to get their teeth into. You'd feel the same yourself. Isn't it a natural and healthy thing to want a bit of roughage? I shouldn't have spoken about design. Design has nothing to do with it. Variety's what they want. Variety and a bit of grit to keep the bowels moving.'

'Thanks,' said the woman in the cap, 'but all the same your husband's wrong about blanks. It's not blanks they want. It's dashes. Here you are: LEAVE A LINE WHERE *not* APPLICABLE.'

'Well do it then,' said the man. 'It's all the same in the end.'

'Not quite,' said his wife. 'A dash is something where a blank is nothing. You still feel you're something if you're making dashes. They've got to see you. You're still *there*. Blanks are just holes, and I've a horror of empty holes. I feel I might drop out of sight forever.'

'I'm not fussy either way,' said the woman. 'But I think I'll put a dash after every five or so as your husband suggested. That'll be enough for a start.'

Section Two was longer than Section One and it grew every minute, for the woman pulled it up and marked it with her right hand and pushed it away with her left as rapidly as it came up from the side of the chair she was sitting on. It seemed she was giving birth to an endless ream of sterile paper, but she kept doggedly on until the paper fell down over the side of the table and was momentarily lost in the folds of the cloth. And now it swung out over the floor and crept forward until at last it became visible on the scruffy brown matting, where it was ruffled a little in the draught from the door which opened and shut continually. It was five o'clock and there were a lot of people around. Occasionally a shoe would scrape the paper and cause the owner to stare down for an instant, or the paper would loop about an ankle and be kicked impatiently aside in the search for seats. It travelled slowly but surely in stiff loops and swathes. One woman whipped it out of her path on the point of an umbrella and it landed round the leg of the table where two elderly gentlemen were solicitously unpicking the flesh from the backs of haddocks. There was a complaint.

'Look madam,' said one of the older waitresses coming across to the woman in the red cap. 'I have a complaint from that table across there. I think you ought to withdraw that paper—or better still, please stop playing whatever it is you're playing. Because one complaint leads to another, and there's a few here beginning to get annoyed. There are places for that kind of thing and this is not one of them. Now do you mind?'

'If she doesn't mind, I do,' said the married man at once. 'It's no game. She's filling up an official form.'

'Well, if it's official why doesn't she do it in an official place?'

'Because,' said the man, 'she's wanting to take time over it. Because it's a more important form than most. Some of those questions, you may have noticed, have double black lines under them. It's not the sort of thing you can do in five minutes standing at the corner of a counter. This woman happens to be doing her duty as you'd have seen if you'd taken the trouble to look.'

'That's absolutely right,' came the brisk voice of a girl leaning backwards from a nearby table—an efficient-looking person who by a coincidence was herself making marks in an open exercise book with her elbow on a pile of others. She was correcting errors of grammar with strong red strokes and errors of taste with pale question marks. 'That's right. I've been watching her. It's a poor show if people are to be scolded and chivied simply for being conscientious. Yes, I've had my eye on her ever since she came in. She's taking a lot of time and trouble over that form. Why should she be interfered with? It's a bit of hard work like any other, and she's a woman just like myself. It isn't as though she were sitting there writing poetry or something!'

The woman in the red cap sat stubbornly silent over the form, waiting for the talk to die down. The waitress flounced round in the crackle of paper around her legs and made off to the other end of the room. The complainers at the opposite side glared and shifted and finally turned their heads away and got on with the backbone picking.

'I've nearly finished Section Two,' said the woman in the red cap, 'though you may not have noticed.'

'Yes, I did notice,' said the wife, 'and I think it's amazing what you've managed to do in spite of everything. What have you got to do next?'

'Wait a minute though—before you go any further,' said the man. 'Haven't you made it too negative? That stroke you've been making almost amounts to "no" or "never" or "don't know" or "haven't got one" or "didn't like him" or "haven't been there" or "couldn't eat it".'

'Was it you who went on about dashes?' said the woman.

'I said every five or so. I'm inclined to think you've overdone it. A varied look is what you're aiming at. Not a negative one.'

'Well, it's too late to change it now.'

'Not at all,' said the one who was still listening at the next table. 'I've got an ink eraser here in my handbag.'

'You must excuse me,' said the man. 'But our friend here knows what she's about. She's filling it up in Indian Ink as she's been instructed. If you start trying to erase black ink you'll rub right through to the table in no time. This isn't one of your pencil and Biro jobs.'

'Is that right?' said his wife. 'Then it's for keeps is it?'

'For filing—yes. But not just ordinary filing. There'll be a photostat of this. It'll change into an entirely different substance.'

'It's for posterity, then?'

'It's here to stay, yes. The writing won't fade and the paper won't wear out.'

'Good for her. Better than manuscripts in the British Museum.'

'In its final form it goes into steel boxes inside steel drawers and into steel cabinets inside steel cupboards. Most places have steel rooms too, though you can't absolutely count on it.'

'Better than the Pharaohs' tombs!'

'Oh, give her some peace to get on with it. How *are* you getting on?' he said to the woman in the cap.

She was looking at Section Three now. She looked at it long and steadily with her head bent close and only her eyes moving back and forth along the heavy black lines of instruction.

'This must be the personal bit coming now,' she said at last. 'It says: JUST ANSWER YES OR NO IN THE BOX PROVIDED.'

'Good. Well, better get on with it then.'

'I'm beginning now. I think I'll start with a YES.'

'Look,' said the man. 'Don't bother with what I said about too many negatives. It doesn't apply in this Section. They just want you to answer as freely and truthfully as possible. If you want to put NO just go ahead. Or YES if you like. Put the whole of yourself into it. It's *you* they want to know about this time.'

'They do, do they? Well, it's getting warmer, isn't it? I can really spread myself.'

'Well, not exactly,' said the wife. 'Not outside the boxes.'

'But it gives her a choice,' said the man. 'YES or NO. It's

117

not so impersonal. There's the human touch coming in.'

'That's what I said,' murmured the woman in the cap. 'They're getting kind of close, aren't they? In fact, I'm not to answer all of them. Look at this one. A YES doesn't suit this one and a NO looks daft. What would you put there? A question mark would be best.'

'Not at all,' said the man. 'It's they who are asking the questions, not you.'

'Well, I'm to leave that empty meantime. And what's in here?' said the old woman, leaning towards the wife. The two women examined the next question with their heads close. 'A black exclamation mark would suit there,' said the wife with a laugh. 'What a nerve! What a hope! Fancy trying to fit *that* in a box. And a box without a lid at that!'

'Look,' said the husband, leaning back with a hint of disapproval in his voice, 'there's such a thing as co-operation. Maybe it's a Survey. If it's a Survey it's probably meant to help in the long run.'

'Help who?' said the old woman.

'You.'

'No help to me.'

'I said in the long run.'

'I'll be dead in the long run.'

'Then for people like you. People coming after.'

'I don't care if they're before or after or from the shop round the corner. Nobody's like me.'

'Look,' said the man patiently, 'they're not asking questions to gratify their own interest. It's not idle curiosity.'

'Oh my goodness—don't give us that bit!' said his wife. 'As though we don't long for a bit of idle curiosity now and then!'

The woman in the red cap took an extraordinary time over the last Section and the ink got low and thick in the bottle. Sometimes it was necessary to clean out blobs of black which had formed between the splayed nib of the pen. She began to write NO more often than YES. The word had a closed and private face more suited to the time of day. For it was getting late. The customers at the far end of the room had long ago laid aside their complaints with the clean-picked bones, and were waiting for the bill. The supporter at the next table had lost interest. The waitresses were already lining up at the wall with their napkins ready for a chance to flip off the tea crumbs. The lights had gone on and fell directly down on tablecloths showing the ancient stains of tea and coffee, faded as monograms on parchment. But in the street outside it was grey and a wind was hustling the passers-by along at a smarter pace. The man and his wife had been silent a long time, watching the woman, but now they began to stare at their watches.

'Don't forget you left one or two items to be filled up,' said the man. 'Are you nearly finished? Do you want us to fetch the first part for you?'

The woman said nothing until she'd reached the very end of the form. 'No thanks,' she said. 'Start digging up how things were before I'm born—and I'll make a mess of it. My mother's age? She never said when she was born. So why should I try to figure it out now? Just to make her mad? I've even forgotten her middle name. The striped bean ring on her middle finger—yes—but the middle name—that's gone for good. You can help me fold the form. It's got to be folded from this end.'

'All right,' said the man. The couple were getting tired. Their eyes followed the loops and coils of paper without enthusiasm and the wife kept staring from the counter clock to her husband and back again. 'It's pretty late,' he said, 'but we'll help you fold it seeing we helped you fill it up. Sit there and keep hold of that end whatever you do, and don't start to fold till we've got the other end sorted out.'

The couple got up and began to work their way through the close-set tables and along the length of the paper, for the end had got shifted again and now lay in a great heap under the stair leading up to the first floor restaurant. The pair knelt down and started to untangle this heap until at last the man pounced triumphantly and held up an end. At the other end of the room the old woman started to fold. The paper came over the floor to her with a soft whispering sound where the going was easy and a tearing scuttling where it was hard. She folded it until it was the size of a thin white baton, and steadily round and round till it made a fair-sized scroll, and on and round till a monstrous roll grew in her arms, changed shape as she folded, gradually lost its tightness and turned to a soft fat pillow of paper.

The man and his wife followed the last length across and stood by the table watching the woman as she kneaded and patted the dumpy pillow into a neater shape.

'Teas are off!' warned the waitress swerving near.

'We know it,' said the old woman. 'And we're off ourselves.' She heaved herself up and hoisted the roll under her arm.

'I'll help you with that,' said the man.

'I'm to carry it myself,' she said. 'I brought it in and I'll take it out. What's more, I'm to hand it in to that place before it closes.'

'What a weight! exclaimed the wife. 'Better let him help.'

'No,' said the woman. 'Though it seems a sight heavier than it was before. All those crosses and dashes must be iron-plated—the weight it is now.'

'It's the time of day,' said the man. 'Everything's at its densest.'

They made their way slowly towards the door, swung it back and stepped out into the street. Those looking out from the café saw the three persons immediately transformed into strugglers as they plunged into the struggling world outside. The jostling pavement, the strong wind, and a crowd disgorging from the nearby bus station had quickly separated the husband and wife from the woman. They were glimpsed only once again. The couple were being pushed forward, side by side, along the length of the bus queue—both leaning at an angle like dancers, their feet scarcely touching the ground. The woman in the red cap was waiting to cross the road with a crowd of others, her eyes fixed on the green GO light which had momentarily turned the wet street into a choppy green and black stream, her two arms hugging the roll of paper in case the wind should tear a strip from it before she could reach the other side.

The waitresses, their arms crossed, were now looking blankly from the windows of the café along with the manageress and a couple of customers who were putting on their coats at the door.

'I must say I think it's rather a disgrace,' said the manageress. 'Any time I've had to fill up a form I've managed to keep it to myself, even if I've had to wind it round and round my body. I've even managed to bind myself from waist to neck in paper—still leaving my hands free to write of course—and that takes a bit of doing. But I don't mind. I'd rather live in a winding-sheet than spread myself as that lot did!'

Allergy

The new lodger glanced down briefly at the plate which had just been put in front of him and turned towards the window with a faint smile, as though acknowledging that the day was fair enough outside, even if there was something foul within.

'I can't take egg. Sorry.'

'Can't take?' Mrs Ella MacLean still kept her thumb on the oozy edge of a heap of scrambled yellow.

'No. It's an allergy.'

'It doesn't agree?'

'No. It's an allergy.'

'Oh, one of those. That's interesting! But you could take a lightly-boiled egg, couldn't you?'

'No, it's an allergy to egg.'

'You mean *any* egg?'

'Any and every egg, Mrs MacLean. In all forms. Egg is poison to me.' Harry Veitch did not raise his voice at all, but this time his landlady withdrew the plate rather quickly. She put it on one side and sat down at the other end of the table.

'Yes, that *is* interesting,' she said. 'I've known the strawberries and the shellfish and the cat's fur. And of course I've heard of the egg, though I've never met it.' Veitch said nothing. He broke a piece of toast. 'No, I've never met it.

Though I've met eggs disagreeing. I mean really disagreeing!'

Veitch was pressing his lips with a napkin. 'Not the same thing,' he said. 'When I say poison I mean poison. Pains. Vomiting. And I wouldn't like to say what else. Violent! Not many people understand just *how* violent!'

Flickers of curiosity alternated with prim blankness in Mrs MacLean's eyes. 'And aren't there dusts and pollens—horse's hair and that sort of thing?'

'All kinds. I don't even know the lot. But they're not all as *violent*.'

There was a silence while Mrs MacLean with a soft white napkin gently, gently brushed away the scratchy toast-crumbs which lay between them in the centre of the table.

'Do you find people sympathetic then?' she enquired at last.

Veitch gave a short laugh. 'Mrs MacLean—when, may I ask, have people ever been sympathetic to anything out of the ordinary?'

'I suppose that's true.'

They both turned their heads to look out onto the Edinburgh street, already crowded with people going to work. There was a stiffish breeze—visitors from the south, like Veitch, used the word 'gale'—and those going eastwards had their teeth bared against it and their eyes screwed up in a grimace which made them appear very unsympathetic indeed. On the pavement below their window, a well-dressed man stooped in the swirling dust to unwind a strip of paper which had wrapped itself round his ankle like a dirty bandage. They heard his curse even with the window shut. This sudden glimpse of the cruelly grimacing human beings, separated from them only by glass, gave them a stronger sense of the warmth within. Human sympathy too. Mrs MacLean was a widow. It was a street of windows—some of them old and grim, living at street level between lace curtains and brown pots of creeping plants, some of them young and gay behind high window boxes where the hardiest flowers survived the Scottish summer. Mrs MacLean was neither of these. She was an amiable woman in her middle years, and lately she had begun to wonder whether sympathy was not her strongest point.

In the weeks that followed Veitch's status changed from lodger to paying guest, from paying guest, by a more subtle transformation shown only in Mrs MacLean's softer expression and tone of voice, to a guest who, in the long run, paid. They talked together in the mornings and evenings. Sometimes they talked about his work which was in the refrigerating business. But as often as not the conversation veered round to eggs. As a subject the egg had everything. It was brilliantly self-contained and clean, light but meaty, delicate yet full of complex far-reaching associations— psychological, sexual, physiological, philosophical. There was almost nothing on earth that did not start off with an egg in some shape or form. And when they had discussed eggs in the abstract Veitch would tell her about all those persons who had tried their best to poison him, coming after him with their great home-made cakes rich with egg, boggy egg puddings nourishing to the death, or the stiff drifts of meringue topping custards yellow as cowslip. It was all meant kindly, no doubt, yet how could one be sure? After all, he'd never made any secret of it. But people who called themselves human were continually dropping eggs here and there into his life as deliberately as anarchists depositing eggs of explosive into unsuspecting communities.

'You'd be amazed,' he said. 'Even persons who profess to love one aren't above mixing in the odd egg—just to test, just to make absolutely certain one isn't trying it on.'

'Oh heavens— Oh no!' cried Mrs MacLean. 'Love! Love in one hand and poison in the other!'

'That's just about it,' Veitch agreed. 'With my chemical make-up you get to know a lot about human nature, and sometimes the things you learn you'd far, far rather never have known.'

By early spring Mrs MacLean and her lodger were going out together in his car on a Saturday, sometimes to a quiet tea-room on the outskirts of the city or further out into the country where they would stretch their legs for a bit before having a leisurely high tea in some small hotel where, as often as not, Mrs MacLean would inform waitresses and sometimes waiters about Harry Veitch's egg allergy. Then Veitch would sit back and watch the dishes beckoned or waved away, would hear with an impassive face the detailed discussions of what had gone into the make-up of certain pies and rissoles, and would occasionally see Mrs MacLean reject a bare-faced egg outright. He never entered into such discussions. It almost seemed as though he had let her take over the entire poisonous side of his life. On the whole, he seemed to enjoy the dining-room dramas when all heads would turn and silence fall at the sound of Mrs MacLean's voice rising above the rest: 'No, no, it's poison to him! Not at all—boiled, scrambled, poached—it's all the same. Poison!' But once in a while the merest shadow of irritation would cross his face, and on some evenings he drove home almost in silence, a petulant droop to his lips.

'But you did enjoy your supper, didn't you?'

'Quite.'

'And you didn't mind me saying that about the egg?'

'Why should I?'

'You see, I actually saw them through the door—whipping it up—even after I'd warned them. Even after I'd told them it was actual poison to you. They were whipping it up in a bowl—with a fork.'

'Exactly.'

'What do you mean—"exactly"?'

'I mean your description is obviously correct.'

'How stilted you make it sound. Why don't you relax—make yourself comfy?'

'While I'm driving? You want me to relax into this ditch for instance?' Very touchy he could be, almost disagreeable at times. But then he was allergic, wasn't he? A sensitive type.

Before long Mrs MacLean had given up eating eggs herself. She wouldn't actually say they disagreed with her nowadays. That would be carrying it too far. But how could what was poison to him be nourishment to her? She hardly noticed when the usual invitations to suppers with neighbours began to dwindle under her too vivid descriptions of eggs and their wicked ways. She was too busy devising new, eggless dishes for Veitch. By early summer she and her guest had explored the surrounding countryside and every out-of-the-way restaurant in the city. Mrs MacLean gave him a great deal. It was not only his stomach she tended. She gave him bit by bit, but steadily and systematically, the history of Edinburgh as they went about. 'You're standing on History!' she would exclaim, nudging him off a piece of paving-stone. Or, as he stood wedged momentarily in the archway of a close on a wild afternoon, her voice would rise triumphantly above the howlings and whistlings around him: 'You're breathing in History! Look at that inscription above your head!' He would step up cautiously onto slabs of wintry stone from which famous clerics had declaimed, sit in deep seats where queens had sat, while Mrs MacLean held forth herself. All the teaching experience of her younger days came back to her as she talked, and often when tourists were around a small crowd would gather and ask questions. One or two Americans might jot down her answers in notebooks and occasionally a photo was taken of her standing in the doorway of St Giles or with one elbow laid nonchalantly on the parapet of the Castle Esplanade. Sometimes Veitch got lost. He got lost for hours and hours, and after much searching Mrs MacLean would have to return home alone. It took a lot out of her. At times History really hurt.

By late autumn Veitch had got his job well in hand. It was expanding, he said. Really bursting its bounds. Mrs MacLean knew little about his job, but she identified with it and she was not one to stand in the way of his work. When he spoke of expansion and bursting bounds, however, refrigeration was the last thing she had in mind, but rather some mature and still seductive woman bursting through all the freezing restrictions into a boundless new life. But she felt a difference. He was not so available now. He worked late and had little appetite for the original eggless dishes she set before him at supper. Worst of all, when a few days of unexpected Indian Summer began, a sudden spate of work took him away from her for longer and longer sessions. He began to be busy on Saturday afternoons, and even on Sundays he found he must use the car to make certain contacts he'd had no time for during the week. Reluctantly, Mrs MacLean decided that until the pressure of work slackened she would simply take a few bus trips on her own while the weather lasted. She set off, good-naturedly enough, on solitary sprees at the week-ends—as often as not ending up with tea alone in some country hotel or seaside café where they had been earlier in the year. She still had supper and breakfast talks with her lodger, but mostly it was herself talking to keep her spirits up. She never mentioned History now. Egg-talk was also out. In the bleak evenings she secretly yearned for the buttery omelettes and feathery soufflés she had whipped up in the old days.

One Saturday afternoon she took the bus right out into the country to an old farmhouse where they had been a couple of months ago. It stood well back from the road amongst low, gorse-covered hills, and winding through these were deep paths where you could walk for miles in a wide circle, eventually coming out again near the house. Mrs MacLean decided to take her walk after tea. There was nobody in the place but her spirits were rather higher than usual. She ate haddocks in egg sauce, pancakes, scones and plum jam and as she ate she talked on and off to the friendly girl who served it. She even managed to bring in a reference to a great friend of hers who was unable to eat egg in any shape or form, and for a while they discussed the peculiarities of people and their eating habits. Then she set off for her walk.

It was one of the last warm days of the year—so warm that after half an hour or so she had to remove her coat, and a mile further on uphill she was glad to lean on a gate and look down to where, far off, she could just see the line of the Crags and Arthur's Seat with the blue haze of the city beneath. Near at hand the weeds of the fields and ditches were a bright yellow, yet creamed here and there in the hollows with low swathes of ground-mist. But something jerked her from her trance. She realized with a shock that she was not the only person enjoying the surroundings.

Unseen, yet close to her behind the hedge, there were human rustlings and murmurings. She bent further over the gate and craned her head sideways to look. Seated on a tartan rug which came from the back of her own drawing-room sofa was Harry Veitch, his arm round the waist of a young woman whose hair was yellow as egg yolk. Their legs lay together, the toes of their shoes pointed towards one another, and Mrs MacLean noted that under a dusting of seeds and straws Veitch's shoes still bore traces of the very shine she had put there the night before. For a few seconds longer she stood staring. From the distance of a field or two away it would have seemed to any onlooker that these three persons were peacefully enjoying the last moments of an idyllic afternoon together. Then, Mrs MacLean suddenly lifted her hands from the top of the gate as though it had been electrically wired, turned swiftly and silently down the way she had come and made for the bus route back to the city.

Sunday breakfast had always been a more prolonged affair than on other days, and the next morning Harry Veitch came downstairs late in green and white striped pyjamas under a maroon dressing-gown. He looked at ease, and on his forehead was a faint glow which was nothing more nor less than the beginning and end of a Scottish sunburn. For the weather had broken. Mrs MacLean greeted him, seated sideways at the table as usual to show that she had already eaten. But now Veitch was showing a strange hesitation in lowering himself into his seat. For some moments he seemed to find extraordinary difficulty in removing his gaze from the circumference of the plate before him, as though its rim were magnetic to the eyes which, try as they might to burst aside, were kept painfully riveted down dead on its centre. But at last, with tremendous effort, he managed to remove them. Casually, smiling, he looked round the room at curtains, pot-plant, firescreen, sideboard—greeting them first before he spoke. And when he spoke it was in an equable voice, polite and low-pitched.

'Mrs MacLean, I can't take egg. Sorry.'

'Can't take?' There was a cold surprise in her voice. Veitch allowed himself one darting glance at the smooth boiled egg on his plate and another at the mottled oval of his landlady's face, and again let his eyes roam easily about the room.

'No, it's an allergy,' he said.

Mrs MacLean now got up with the teapot in her hand and poured out a cup for her lodger. 'I don't quite catch your meaning, Mr Veitch,' she said, coming round and standing with the spout cocked at his ear as though she would pour the brown brew into his skull.

'An allergy, Mrs MacLean,' said Veitch, speaking with the distinct enunciation and glassy gaze of one practising his vocabulary in a foreign tongue. 'I have an allergy to egg.'

'Do you mean you want special treatment here, Mr Veitch?'

'Mrs MacLean, I am allergic to egg. Egg is poison to me. Deadly poison!'

Mrs MacLean's face was blank, her voice flat as she answered:

'Then why should you stay here? In an egg-house.'

'An egg-house!' The vision of a monstrous six-compartment egg-box had flashed before Veitch's eyes.

'Yes, I love eggs,' she replied simply. 'Eggs are my favourite. I shall order two dozen eggs tomorrow. There will be eggs, fresh eggs, for breakfast, for lunch, for supper. Did you know there are ways of drinking eggs? One can even break an egg into the soup for extra nourishment. I have books crammed with recipes specifically for the egg. There are a thousand and one ways ...'

'Poison!' cried Harry Veitch on a fainter note.

'Yes, indeed ... if you stay. A thousand and one ways ...' she agreed. And for a start—with the expression of an irate conjurer—she produced a second boiled egg out of a bowl and nimbly bowled it across the table towards her shrinking lodger.

The High Tide Talker

'I've nothing to take me back! I could stay for hours if I wanted to, or if the weather was anything. All the same, once he starts to talk it's likely to be the same thing as yesterday and the day before.' The woman at the first drops of rain had pushed through to the front of the crowd and now stood close to the balustrade of the promenade, looking down onto the beach. 'You wouldn't call him a good-looker, would you?' she said to the young man beside her. 'But then, he doesn't need to be. Look at his background. Waves and clouds and ships, and sometimes even a sail or two. And no surprise to me if he got a whale spouting before he's through with the place. That's the kind he is. He's lucky. You can say anything as long as the setting's right. Now if there were brass rails and a pulpit round him or maybe an ugly black cloth behind—would you have stopped to hear?' The young man said nothing. 'Or come to that—if he'd black boots on instead of bare feet—would anyone look twice?' Watson, the young man, kept his eyes fixed on the beach. A man on his other side spoke across him to the woman: 'But have you thought of the snags of open-air talking? Gulls can tear the words to bits. Waves can gulp them up. And now he's got the weather to contend with.' But the big, warm splashes of summer rain had come to nothing. The woman who had stepped aside with her umbrella half-open, closed it again. 'Will you come often?' she asked. Watson muttered something and shook his head. But whenever possible these last ten days, he'd been here. He would come tomorrow if he could get away, and the next day and for every day after that, as long as the man below had breath to talk.

The man on the beach was called Carruthers. He was a large man, tall and burly, wearing today a blue cotton jacket and striped grey and brown trousers rolled up at the ankles. On warmer days his shirts were brilliantly flowered and checked, and always, whether it was warm or cool, he had on a large tropic-style straw hat, red-banded, and cut into fronds round the brim's edge. His head when he removed the hat was square and strong with stiff, straw-coloured hair which showed grey at the roots as the wind lifted it. Sometimes he would swing his arms up as he talked and his eyes would follow the green glint of a ring on his finger as it stabbed the air. Very often there was this contrast between the movements of his body and the watchful person who studied himself with interest or listened attentively to the ups and downs of his own voice. He was not always shouting. He would begin every afternoon or evening when the tide was still a good way out and all was quiet on the shore. Each time he would be cut short in full swing by the crash of waves as the tide came up. There was a beginning but never an end to his harangue.

This evening there were not many left on the shore. A few children who had been splashing about in pools far down on the rocks were slowly beginning to move up the beach, but they could still be clearly heard against the soft, rhythmic splashing of the advancing sea. As usual Carruthers began quietly. He hardly needed to raise his voice. It was more like a casual, one-sided conversation as

134

he looked up, smiling, to the group gathered above him on the promenade.

'You're enjoying your holiday, I hope, as much as I'm enjoying mine. You *seem* to be enjoying it. I look up and think: "They haven't a care in the world, that lot", and you look down at me and think: "Look at him. He's strong. He's in good health, isn't he? He's lucky. He's not the worrying kind." But, friends, that's not so. We've all got our worries. Maybe we feel good now. It's still day. But what about the night? It's still fair—but what about the storm? You can still hear birds and children and the cars going along up there on the road. But come down here at midnight as I do sometimes—no, no, not often I admit—but when the tide's full in and it's black, I'm not thinking day thoughts then. I'm thinking night thoughts. They're different, aren't they? I have them and you have them too, even if it's only for two minutes as you're turning over in bed, or just for the time it takes to get to the kitchen and back for a drink of water. But that's enough. It's plenty of time for one or two night thoughts—and heaven help us all, you may say, if we give ourselves much longer than that! All right then. What are these thoughts?' Carruthers drew his hands out of his pockets and the casual air was gone in a flash. His voice dropped. 'We're alone. That's the first thing that comes to mind. But utterly alone. Oh yes, you've got your families. You've got your friends. So have I. Maybe you're lucky enough to have a best friend who comes running when you're in real trouble. But there's some trouble no one can help with. We've all got to die one day and who's to help us then? It doesn't matter if a bishop holds your hand. It doesn't matter if a cardinal's your brother ...'

'This is where he loses me,' said the woman with the

135

umbrella. 'If I've got to strain my ears it had better be cheery. I never stay for the death bit—not in films, not even in books—certainly not on my holiday.' She moved off, pausing further along at a red collection box fixed to the balustrade and inscribed simply with the two words: FOR LIGHT painted in bold white letters.

The man on the beach spoke on for another twenty minutes at least, before he had to start gradually raising his voice above the tide. During that time he varied his performance. Sometimes he waited while a few more joined the group and he drew in the uncertain ones with extravagant, knee-bending beckonings, as though scooping them up from outer space towards his chest. Or he would turn and watch while a gang of jeering rowdies went by below him on the sand. Then he would make as though to sweep up after them by running and driving the sand before him with an invisible broom, brandishing it in the air and finally hurling it after them. When there was nothing better to do he stopped and studied himself from head to foot with interest. Without a word he would move to the promenade wall, roll up a sleeve or a trouser-leg and unbutton his shirt down to the waist. Pointing, twisting, giving himself a pinch or a slap or two, he'd show them the odd scar, a brown burn-mark, a blue bruise here and there. They were nothing at all. Most of his audience had far better marks themselves. Nevertheless the pointing and the pinching got them. They stared, fascinated, over one another's shoulders.

Not so far down the beach the tops of the first line of sandcastles were dissolving, their deep moats swirling. Just above them was a deep ledge of pebbles and as soon as the sea touched this the sound seemed to increase tenfold. Carruthers was not speaking against a mere rise and fall of water but against a grinding rattle of stones growing steadily stronger as the waves drove up into their midst. He looked behind him once or twice to measure his distance. The tide was coming in fast.

'But we've got to die the same as we've got to live!' he called up, circling his mouth with his hands. 'And who or what's to help us? It's a fearsome thought all right. But we *can* escape that fear!' Again Carruthers looked behind and gestured to the sea. 'For instance, you may wonder how I'll escape a wetting if that tide comes in too fast. There are no steps at this bit. But I've got a way up. Not everyone knows about it but I know it's there so I don't worry. We're all going to need an escape, friends. Not for the body, but for the soul. But where will we find this escape? How will we make sure of it?' Carruthers waited for a long time examining the blank wall in front of him. He was not forced to answer. There was a roaring behind and a huge wave came lashing up yards further than the rest and broke over the top of the promenade. Spray covered the group right to the back line. In a moment they were gone. The preacher himself had disappeared along the wall to his secret escape route. Watson was carried off with the rest.

He was carried off with the rest, but as soon as he was free of the group he slowed down. He was no holiday-maker. He had the resident's half-scorn for the September crowd, while at the same time working all out to meet its appetite. The place where he worked was the best butcher shop in town—one which for half a century had supplied the ever-increasing demand of hotels and boarding-houses in the district. It was a large establishment, stretching far back to where the loaded tables stood, their white, scrubbed wood sagging in voluptuous waves under decades of

137

chopping. But the meat had its class and blood distinctions. In the forefront of the shop the better cuts were arranged on frills of paper and thick backgrounds of artificial parsley. Sheets of tissue, fine as chiffon, divided ribs from kidneys, kidneys from livers, livers from tongues, and double thick parcelling made certain that no drop of blood was ever seen in the place. On the other hand the necklets of pink and cream sausages which filled the platters on either side of the counter were treated with a certain disdain. The butchers whipped them up on the points of their knives and held them in the air, waiting impatiently to slit the chain while the customer pondered his order. The main distinction of the place was that unlike other butcher shops whole animals were in evidence. On trestles in an inner room lay sheep, legs stiff in air, while on certain mornings great pink pigs, rippling with wrinkles, were swung head downward from van to shop, their smooth, debristled ears veined with scarlet like leaves of flesh. The pigs were met and escorted in by men in white coats and hats. Such sights as these gave the shop its standing. It was also, for those inside, a viewing point, standing as it did at a busy corner, with its long windows facing out on all sides. Watson had a mixture of pride and hatred for the place. All during the last fortnight he had thought about Carruthers. He had kept a look out for him as he chopped and sawed and knotted. Occasionally he caught a glimpse of him between the hooks of swinging joints, tramping past, head down, alone—and once he followed him for a bit on his way to the beach.

It was difficult to follow Carruthers. His message depended on the sea. Without some knowledge of tides it was easy to miss him. There was even a rumour that he would be gone in a week. But early or late and as often as his work allowed Watson was on the promenade. He was not put off by repeat performances, nor that the final message or answer was always terminated by the tide. To Watson repetition was part of the attraction. What was left unsaid might one day give him his opening. 'Which way should we look for help?' Carruthers kept yelling before the waves crashed. 'Is it here?'—thumping his stomach, 'or out there? Is there anything behind the dust and stars? Any power or reason there? Is this possible?' Watson silently noted the questions and came back for more. He was there to catch Carruthers' eye if need be, to stay hidden or to stand out. All he asked was to be recognized as a follower. There was as yet no sign of recognition.

On Saturday Watson had a free afternoon and as soon as possible he set off for the promenade. But long before he reached it a heavy shower had started and as he approached he met Carruthers' crowd already making for the nearby cafés or hurrying back for entertainment at the town's centre. One or two were still looking expectantly over the balustrade but Carruthers had not waited till they disappeared. He was sitting with his back to the shelter of the wall drawing a pair of rubber boots over thick white socks. His straw hat, protected by a sheet of newspaper, and a light knapsack lay beside him. Watson stood at a distance watching closely until the rain let up a bit, until he saw the man below stand up and put on his hat, button the collar of his jacket and slowly start off along the beach —going eastward to where the distant cliffs began. Only when Carruthers was already some way in front did Watson follow him.

The tide was still fairly far out and it was quiet on the shore. As they walked further and further along, the sand became smoother and deeper. The castles and trenches, the huge, spade-written letters, the stone circles and shell heaps gradually became sparse until at last—far out—they passed one solitary sandpile stuck round with gulls' feathers. It was a lonely fort, defended by a complex system of walls and ditches, yet doomed like all the rest. Carruthers turned his head and gave it a sidelong look as he passed. Behind him Watson plodded on looking neither to right nor left. The footsteps he followed were sunk deep and widely spaced and sometimes he sank his own feet into them. He was disappointed with the boots. He would have preferred to follow bare feet. But as he went on he became reconciled to them. He thought of all the people who had ever followed behind—who had trekked for years after explorers, hacked their way westward, plodded north into ice on the heels of pioneers. He thought of soldiers following leaders, and of all the people beckoned on by guns and torches, crosses and flaming swords. He thought of the single, lonely followers who accompanied hermits at a distance, seconds-in-command who took over from generals, and the patient understudies who stood in at a moment's notice for actors and preachers, taking on fans and followers and paying off the hangers-on. Sometimes Watson stood still and looked back to the complex trail of double footsteps behind, and forward to the single track he followed. And he thought of the appalling complexities and conflicts of followers compared to the single dedication of leaders.

The man in front stopped suddenly, glanced back for a moment and went on again. The beach had begun to curve round and cut off sight of the town. The main shopping street had long since disappeared, and then the big, south-facing hotels. One by one the spaced-out villas went and finally the furthest caravan. In front was a long stretch of black stones and a great gash in the nearest cliff where they had been torn out. Once or twice Watson found his foot jammed between rocks and once he stopped to put on a shoe which had been ripped off. It took longer than he'd bargained for. He had to balance himself at a slant while he tipped out the sand and knotted up the wet laces. When he set off again he had to stop himself breaking into a run on the smoother stretches. This would have looked like pursuit. He was not a pursuer but a follower. Carruthers stopped again, shouted something unintelligible and went on. Watson was used to words being swamped. For all he knew it might have been 'Come on!' or 'Get moving!' He hurried on.

They had now come a long way and again the character of the shore had changed. Instead of black rocks there was now an open stretch of sand in front, covered with grey pebbles. Driftwood was piled under the cliff, stripped trees and bleached green ropes, baskets, and fish boxes with Scandinavian names. And bones. White birdbones, white skulls and the bones of sheep. Everything was blanched here. Momentarily Watson felt himself stripped and bloodless, walking like a ghost amongst cast-offs. He forgot the chunks of red flesh where he worked, the meaty bones and lumps of opaque fat—these were far behind him. He was entering a dimension made transparent by endless wind and sea. He could also see with peculiar clarity what was in front. A long strip of low cloud was lifting and he saw familiar green meadows against black sky—a glassy green today, like the green of thick sea-bottles through which an illusion of great distance can be seen. Watson wasn't looking at the ground now. But the man in front had slowed down and every now and then he stopped

141

to shift something with his foot. Sometimes he picked up a stone or a piece of wood. Watson was close enough now to hear his breathing. Suddenly Carruthers stopped dead and turned round. 'GO ... AWAY!' he shouted, putting slow and blistering emphasis onto both words. Watson stopped, looked wildly round for guidance, and came on. Again the man in front swerved, again he shouted while still moving on and making pushing gestures back with his arms as he walked. Watson saw the fields more transparent than ever through a shimmer of water. He hesitated for an instant, staring at his feet, then plodded on. Carruthers lengthened his stride until there was again a fair distance between them, but after some time he slowed down, finally came to a halt. Grimly, but on a more resigned note, he called back: 'What do you want?' Slowly Watson made up on him. He didn't, however, come right up but approached to within some yards and stopped.

'What do you want?' Carruthers said again. He looked, close-up, unexpectedly tall.

'I have questions,' said Watson. The voice was deferential.

'I can't hear you,' said Carruthers. Watson turned to repudiate this, for the tide was still a good way out. The water was making no more than a gentle splashing on the stones.

'And I don't *want* to hear,' said Carruthers, watching the direction of his eyes. 'If it's the walk you want I can't stop you, can I? But if it's company—I'm not your man. You'd better go back.'

'Dozens of questions,' said Watson, his voice still soft but at the same time stubborn.

Carruthers gave a great shrug of his shoulders and turned. Not far in front was a hollowed out part of the cliff—hardly a cave but deep enough with its overhanging bluff to give shelter. Carruthers made for this. It was obviously known to him. Already he had wedged himself and his stuff into a ledge of rock and was sitting easing off one of his boots when Watson came up and stood discreetly at the opening.

'So this is your place!' he said at last, looking about him with suspicious reverence. Carruthers had taken off his jacket and was rummaging in his bag. 'What do you mean— my place? I'm not a cave-dweller. It's some sort of shelter from the wind when I want to eat.'

'When you want to think,' Watson corrected him. Carruthers sighed. He unwrapped a packet which contained three rolls, a few rings of raw onion, a lump of cheese, tomatoes, and some slices of boiled egg which he put on one side. 'You'd better help yourself,' he said, pointing to the rolls.

'I don't want anything,' said Watson. 'I didn't come for food.'

'Is that so? Then you can watch me eat.' Carruthers brought back the egg slices and started to fill a roll.

'I can go off if you like,' said Watson. 'I can come back when you're finished.'

Carruthers blew sand from the roll's crust. 'Oh, sit down! You worry me standing out there. You'll only shuffle up more sand. Do you think I'm a member of some tribe who's forbidden to eat in public? As a matter of fact I'm perfectly used to eating with dozens, maybe hundreds, staring at me.' He took a bite of the roll and after some time added thoughtfully: 'Under a spotlight too.'

'Spotlight,' Watson repeated. He thought of a sunshaft. Perhaps even moonlight.

'I'm talking, of course, about eating on stage. And the

food was real food. Don't have any misconceptions about that. I could have made a meal of it if I'd wanted to.' Carruthers was reluctantly resigning himself to the young man, but he spoke and ate as though solely for himself. Occasionally he stopped chewing and his eyes warmed as some memory struck him. Watson was staring blankly ahead and Carruthers turned his head for a moment and looked at him. 'You work in that big butcher's shop in town, don't you? I caught sight of you the other day throwing double links of sausages from the end of a knife.' He opened up another roll, packed it with cheese and pressed it down.

'Are you going to say I shouldn't work with meat?' said Watson.

'God—what now! Why should I do that? I was about to congratulate you on a remarkable act.'

'All right. I thought maybe you were a vegetarian, along with everything else.'

'Along with everything else! Look, eat up, for God's sake, and stop staring.'

'I'm not hungry,' said Watson. 'I told you what I'd come for.'

'Oh, yes—questions, of course. What questions? If it's questions about *me* ...'

'No—more than that ...!'

'If it's about me,' Carruthers went on, ignoring this, 'that's easy. There's only one thing to tell. I've already mentioned it. I'm a theatre man, first and always—and very proud of it too,' he added as he watched Watson's face. 'That is, of course whenever the job's there. When the job's *not* there, when the curtain's down too long, that is, in the spare time—amongst other things—I'm a preacher. For the fun of it.'

'Fun!' Watson turned at last a bleak and harrowed face.

144

'Or for the hell of it, if you'd rather.' Carruthers watched the movement of Watson's mouth and eyebrows with professional interest. 'I'd hesitate,' he said, 'to call myself an actor pure and simple. And I have my pantomime parts of course—not unlike that sausage act of yours. You've got the basis there, I may say, for one or two passable turns.'

Now the silence between them lasted a long time—so long that in the interval the sea had come a few yards further up the beach. It had taken back the heaped-up seaweed and was advancing upon the lowest line of driftwood before Carruthers spoke again. He'd taken some cake from an outside pocket of his bag and was settling down to eat it, his legs stretched out comfortably, his eyes on the horizon. 'Think of it,' he said, waving one hand at the water, 'all those layers upon layers of creatures out there, munching for their lives—nibbling, sucking, sieving through the water for sustenance. Eating and being eaten. And not a speck wasted!'

'I know all that,' said Watson in a stifled voice, 'and I don't want to hear. Your job ...'

'Right. What *is* my job, in your opinion?'

'Your job's to say what's in it all for *us*! Who cares what's in the sea? It's what goes on above ...' Watson signalled to the sky. Carruthers slapped his hand down on a rock. 'Will you listen to him!' he exclaimed softly to the invisible shoals.

'I'm the listening one! You saw me. Every free minute, I was down. Every day for the last fortnight ...'

'I didn't ask you. You came of your own accord, and you're as free to go.'

Carruthers had produced a can of beer and through the hiss and bubble of its opening he remarked with satisfaction: 'There's only one of these. You'll have to watch this time. You see, I wasn't prepared for a picnic.' Watson watched him drink. He drank extravagantly, the knob in his throat frisking. 'You may well ask "what goes on above?"' he said at last setting the can down. 'Unbelievable things go on. Fantastic blow-outs, spinnings and explosions—wholesale drop-outs, stars, groups of galaxies, groups of groups ... you want me to go on? We're still as ignorant of it all as cheese mites about chess, but look— we're getting *some*where, aren't we? You might say, and without stretching a point, the curiosity is whetted!' Carruthers glanced at Watson. 'Or again you might not.' He fell silent, but after a time he took the ring off his finger and held it up. 'I've another like this,' he said watching Watson out of the corner of his eye. 'Both of them gifts. I've also a gold watch—another gift—which I don't always care to wear. This cheap one does well enough on trips. Time, on seaside shows, counts for nothing. In the theatre, on the other hand, it's everything.' He took another drink and leaned back with the bag propping his shoulders. A strange sound came from Watson's throat as he watched.

'Who was I listening to—up there?' he cried suddenly in an anguished voice.

'Who? Up there on the prom? Why me, of course. Charles Quentin Carruthers.'

'Player or preacher?'

'Both, both! What's the matter with the mixture?' Carruthers sat forward and studied himself. 'I can turn my hand to most things,' he said. 'In the early days I've even taken on conjuring, sandwiched between the usual roles— detective, maniac, grandee, and the like. I've actually stood in for a singer, and no one was any the wiser in that town. Go on. Look hard. Look as long as you like! You may have met, for once in your life, the genuine all-round,

146

all-purpose man.' Watson needed no telling. He had his head turned over his shoulder, grimacing as though his neck hurt him. 'But are you a believer?' he said.

'Oh, I'm a believer all right. Don't worry. I'll believe in anything you care to name—as long as it works. Do you want a list of beliefs?'

'Are you a believer?' Watson said again, without turning his head. Even so his neck seemed to pain him, for his face grew pale. For a long time there was no sound in the cave. Then Carruthers got slowly to his feet, turned in towards the cliff face and stretched up so that his fingertips just touched the bulge of rock above him. He seemed to enjoy the sensation so much so that it was prolonged and the stretch became an effort to put the palms of both hands on the rock. Now he straddled his legs and swung forward, easing his back down and down until his knuckles scraped the stones between his feet. Watson darted a look behind and saw through Carruthers' shirt the knobbed line of his spine and the fringe of grey hair flopping behind his hands.

'I believe,' Carruthers was muttering to himself as he came up, 'in a bit of exercise—the smallest thing is better than nothing at all. How else could I have mastered all the movements I've had to make on stage—including falling, fainting, dying?' Watson glanced behind him once again and shuddered. Carruthers had flopped to the ground and was rolling in a boneless bundle on the sharp stones, knees drawn up, hands clasping head. 'Unhurt!' he said, looking up with a grin. Watson turned away quickly as he got to his feet. Carruthers began to stuff his things back into his bag, picking up the odd scraps and wrapping them in newspaper. He went after the beercan which had rolled to the opening. 'I believe in keeping the place decent,' he remarked as he went past Watson, 'whether it's a house or a cave—every last scrap. You'll not find a trace of me wherever I've been. And clothes. Yes, I know how to keep my clothes looking good, and what's more, how to wear them. I've never been a one to be part of the props or the background. Never.'

Watson was breathing fast and sitting tight as ever. 'Have you finished then?' he asked, '—All the things you can do?' Leaning against the rock-face Carruthers studied Watson—from his decent lacing shoes to the hard knot of the throttling tie at his throat. There was a squeamish mixture of modesty and pride about the man. 'I like a bit of glitter in my own get-up, I must say,' said Carruthers, 'even if it's only the odd button. People like a show and I believe in showing off. There's no place for modesty or hanging back in my trade.' He waited for a reply and getting none went on: 'People like a fright now and then. I believe in giving it to them. Sometimes when they're properly scared they'll cheer and clap. Make it easy and you'll get chased. I believe in keeping on the move. Never the same place twice if you can help it. Never the same crowd.'

Watson was beginning to recover himself. There was something lighter and smoother about him now, as though to allow as much of Carruthers' talk to slide off him as possible. He had slicked down his hair and buttoned his jacket to the neck. He sat with his legs drawn up under him, his hands tucked in his sleeves. 'You have a box,' he said. 'A collecting box.'

'Which I'm not ashamed of,' said Carruthers quickly. 'I believe in making the odd pound or two any way I can— talking or standing on my head if need be. But for all that I *believe* in what I'm saying. I'm not a hoaxer or a swindler.' He was preparing to leave. He rolled down his sleeves, adjusting the cuffs carefully, put on his jacket and pulled a red and black spotted scarf from the pocket. Lastly he picked up the straw hat and put it on. 'I believe in myself,' he said. He went past the small figure at the cave's opening and out onto the beach.

Carruthers began striding back purposefully in the direction he had come. He didn't look round, for Watson was behind, limping a bit now in his thin shoes and going cautiously. But when Carruthers stopped he stopped, when Carruthers moved on he moved on. The distance he kept between them was always the same, exact enough to be measured with a rule. They'd gone a hundred yards or so when Watson climbed on a rock and shouted: 'I've found your weakness!'

Carruthers stopped and turned. He walked back a little way. 'Don't follow me,' he called out. 'Walk in front or beside if you must. I won't be followed.'

'I can't do that,' Watson called back. 'I'm coming after you, whatever you are.' Again Carruthers strode ahead, quickening the pace, and Watson quickened his steps and kept his distance.

'I've found your weakness!' he shouted again after a few minutes. Carruthers turned and waited for him to come up. 'And I'm not the only one,' said Watson when he was within a yard or two. He was breathing quickly as though he'd been running along behind. 'Others have noticed. Weakness is the wrong word!' Carruthers shrugged his shoulders and walked on, but behind Watson was shouting: 'It's a trick, isn't it? You've been on it for weeks, maybe months. Have you been playing it for years?' Again Carruthers waited for him to come within speaking distance. 'Right—you tell me,' he said, 'tell me about this trick, this weakness you've discovered.' Watson was still breathing fast. There was a twist to the upper part of his body, as though he could as easily run back as come on. 'You've worked out your tide-times cleverly,' he said, 'for I've come at all ungodly hours to hear you—morning, afternoon and evening. Oh, yes, you put the questions all right, but there's never an answer. You make sure of that. Do you ever reach the end of that sermon of yours? No, because long before you've reached the point the waves come up.'

'What point?' said Carruthers.

'You know what point.'

'I'm asking you. What point?' said Carruthers.

'The God bit.'

'Is that all?' The smile accompanying these words goaded Watson to a frenzy. There was good nature in it, plus a hint of scorn.

'All! We don't get God. We don't get heaven, never mind hell. You leave a gap. You leave a blank. You're off, of course, before the trouble starts. Where are your pamphlets, by the way? There's not one placard in the town. Why not? Well I can tell you why not. Question marks are all you could chalk up. And you can laugh!'

With one hand Carruthers slowly wiped the smile from his face and flipped it behind him. 'Anything more?'

'Yes.'

'You want to prove something?'

'Yes.'

'To test something?'

'You.'

'Try it then.'

'Give your talk tomorrow.'

'I mean to. With no encouragement from you, thanks all the same.'

'Give it when the tide's out! Give it when it's so far out you can neither see nor hear it from the prom.'

Carruthers face didn't change. 'So you're to give me my cues? Dictating times and places.'

'Will you or won't you?'

'Will I what?'

'Preach on the beach when the tide's out?'

For a split second Carruthers hesitated. 'If that's what you want, it's all the same to me. I can do it anywhere and at anytime. You can have me hanging from the edge of the cliff, if you like it that way.'

'Low tide tomorrow!' shouted Watson.

'Low tide. 6.48 p.m. I'll be there.' Carruthers' eyes narrowed and fixed Watson against his background of slippery stones. 'But seeing we're bargaining—you dare to follow after me just one more step on this beach, and I'll make it bad for you, Watson. Stay by your rock. Don't lift that foot! One move from you before I'm off this beach ...!' Carruthers made off, his head sideways towards the cliff so that without turning round he could still note Watson's smallest move.

Watson stayed where he was. His legs felt weak and after a bit he sat down, still with his gaze fixed on Carruthers as he moved further and further along the shore. Each step he marked, as though, reduced to following him faithfully only with his eyes, he made these eyes as far-reaching, as vindictive and demanding as human eyes could be.

The following day was cold, but the haze was gone. Every near object stood in the sun with a sharp shadow. Even the waves had a flashing, cutting edge. It was a day corresponding exactly to Watson's mood. He had recovered his spirits, and from early morning he felt the scourging, purging strength in him grow. It was a busy day. All

151

morning, with gift-wrapping care, he folded and tied up slices of pork and beef. Between cuts he sharpened the long knives and deftly trimmed the fat from the rims of steaks, as though cutting off the last superfluous scraps of sloth from his own day. He grew quicker and surer as the time wore on. At four-thirty he was scouring the tables in the back room as though washing blood from marble. By six he was washed and dressed and sitting by himself in one of the small cafés along the front. He ate little but he watched everyone who passed the window, and when there was a gap in the passers-by he watched the sea. The tide was a very long way out. Below the seaweed line a great expanse of beach shelved down—dangerously steep in places—criss-crossed with rivulets. All along the foreshore lay large black pools which gradually diminished in the distance till they were mere discs of light. It was his own shore, yet for all that, almost unknown. He had never studied it at low tide. The jagged tops and miniature chasms of unfamiliar rocks took his eye. From where he sat he could see, on the dry band of sand under the promenade, a few figures diminished and darkened against the shining slopes behind. Watson bent forward and glanced along the length of the promenade to the semi-circular balustrade which overlooked the beach. There was always a small crowd gathered here staring at the posters advertising evening cruises or queuing at the ice-cream and hot-dog vans. At twenty past six he fixed his eyes on this spot and remained rigid, his forehead touching the window, his feet uncomfortably trapped between wainscot and tilted chair. At six-thirty, as though twitched by a distant cord, his head jerked back, the chairlegs stabbed the floor and he was on his feet. Above the aimless shift of heads he had caught a glimpse of a red-banded straw hat moving slowly towards the balustrade.

Carruthers had taken up his stance on the beach by the time Watson arrived. He had his arms crossed, his feet were planted wide apart with his hat between them and he waited, smiling, for the crowd to form along the balustrade above. They were not long in gathering for any evening show. Already there were a fair number when Watson came up and he had to wedge himself in near the back. He was not sorry to be hidden. The unaccustomed silence of low tide was stunning, in spite of a cutting little breeze coming off the sea. Watson noted with surprise and satisfaction how small Carruthers looked against the space behind. The man had lost half his stature even before opening his mouth. When he did begin to speak his voice was conversational as usual. And Watson smiled. For so it would remain. This time the sea could never save the day. Drama had been killed for the man. He edged in to listen.

'I hope you're enjoying your holiday,' said Carruthers taking in the group with a glance. 'I know I'm enjoying mine.' There was a slight murmuring amongst the crowd and a brief titter. The day had been cold from the start and gradually, throughout late afternoon, all brightness had been overcast. Nylons were being changed for wool. For the first time that season the long-term forecast was poor.

'And you're right,' said Carruthers, quick to take his cue. 'One minute it's fair, the next it's dark. We don't know what's to come.'

'But you'll tell us!' called a voice from the back. There was a sudden parting in the group and heads turned round towards Watson who was dodging down again behind the shoulders. He was known to many as a faithful listener.

His words might be no more than simple statement of fact. There were some who had their doubts.

'Certainly I'll tell you,' said Carruthers easily and with a cool glance in Watson's direction. 'Some questions, of course, aren't answered as easily as all that. Some take a while. Some take a bit of looking into. We'll be coming to those in a minute.'

Watson was heard to laugh. 'And some never get answered at all,' he murmured to those nearest him.

'We've all chosen this fantastic place!' Carruthers swung round, gesticulating towards the eastern cliffs, then to the west with its series of sandy bays, and pointing above him to the winding streets which climbed up steeply behind the crowd. 'We all know why we're here in this town. That's one thing we're clear about. You decided to come and I decided—weeks, maybe months ago. We made up our minds. Right?'

'Not me, chum. It's my missis makes up *my* mind,' said a stout man near the front who was holding a bulging carrier bag.

'We all know why we're here,' Carruthers went on. 'Do we ever ask how we came to be on this globe? Why we're in the universe at all?'

'No. It's you who's to tell us!' called the angry voice from behind. The conviction had now grown strong that Watson must have reason for his change of heart. There was an impatient fidgeting round the edges of the group.

'Who, or what force put us here, and why?' said Carruthers. He paused for a moment to put up the collar of his jacket. 'It may be we're still young with plenty of gumption, or maybe we're on our last legs—but whatever the way of it, we'll always ask questions. One day we're going to need a few answers.'

154

'Get on with it then!' someone shouted.

'Ay, better buck up. You're getting gey long in the tooth yourself,' said an old man. Carruthers' lips were set in a smile unlike his usual flash of teeth. He now doubled over and gave himself a sharp thrashing around the ribs under pretext of warming up. There was a hiss from somewhere in the crowd, soft and poisonous as escaping gas.

'He doesn't know how to go on,' murmured a woman holiday-maker who'd been watching with narrowed eyes. 'Give him another ten minutes and I reckon he'll dry up.' The man beside her held up a finger to his lips: 'Sh ... we're getting answers soon, don't you worry. He'll tie it all up tonight. Right now he's working up to it. Take a look at his face.'

'Who cares?' said a young man who was simply passing through the crowd on his way to a block of boarding-houses at the other end of the town. 'Don't give me answers! No one opens his mouth these days but he's got an answer inside, all smooth and pat as a new-laid egg at the wrong end.' He elbowed his way through and carried on purposefully between a long line of seats which had quickly emptied as the air grew cold.

The man on the beach was still speaking in his normal voice, for apart from the occasional plop in the pools and the squawk of a seagull swooping down to study the shore, there was almost no sound at all. Once in a while Carruthers looked over his shoulder as though expecting some crashing backstage cue to help. None came. There was emptiness behind. 'Look,' said Carruthers. 'Here we are gathered together from every corner of the land. And I've got questions to put to you.'

'Hell ... no ...' murmured the fat man with the carrier,

though in a genial voice. 'You got it wrong! It's you telling *us*.'

'The fact is,' said Watson, edging in from the back and turning his head about to catch the attention on every side, 'the man's just a high-tide talker. He can't do his thing now. He's flummoxed. I think we've had it. I think we can all go home.' A sudden bluster of icy wind gave point to his words. There was a buttoning up followed by a resolute jangling as a woman held up a bangled hand. 'No, I'm not leaving till I get one or two straight answers!'

'Thank you madam.' Carruthers bowed. 'And I mean to give them. Though don't count on them being dead straight.' There was a reproving shuffling above him, some hoots and a thin burst of clapping. 'I'll bet,' murmured the fat man, still genial.

'Let's look at it,' said Carruthers. 'Straight? You can't get it that way. Show me one straight thing. Not a cell in the body. Not an atom in the air or in the sea. In the entire universe—just give me one straight thing!'

'Never mind all that. What I asked for was a straight answer.' The woman was hammering the air with her arm. 'It's about time God was brought into it!'

'Ay ... high time,' her husband agreed.

'I'm coming to that!' Carruthers was shouting now. He split his legs wide apart, reached for the largest pebble beside his foot and hurled it back between his thighs. It ricocheted from one rock, smashed onto another and fell into a pool. They heard the far-off splash in silence.

'He's got to get to the God bit now,' murmured Watson looking about him with a smile. 'Watch it. He can't get round it. No amount of tricks, acrobats or anything else is going to help. He's in trouble. If you want my opinion, I don't believe he's got the smallest clue.'

It was now so cold that even the couple in the hot-dog van had closed down the hatch and could be seen through the rear window lighting up over newspapers in the back. High up on the miniature fairfield above the town red and yellow flags were fluttering and a procession of small round clouds moved in very low, like navy blue balloons, above the bunting.

Down on the beach Carruthers had his hat on and was trying to hold its frondy brim down on both sides. His eyes when he raised his chin again looked belligerent. His face was red. There was a feeling that next time a stone might fly either way. 'I'm here,' he said, 'ready to pronounce on any bloody, mortal thing you care to name! But at my own time! It's still my show— remember?'

'Oh ... ay. Any *mortal* thing,' said the fat man, smiling round in a friendly fashion. 'That's easy. No trouble. I'd be glad enough to speak on any *mortal* thing myself. Though that wasn't what was called for, was it?'

Carruthers was looking through the fat man as though willing him to transparency. 'I'm all ready,' he said again, 'to talk of powers, of forces if you like, natural or supernatural, atom-smashing forces, star-blasting, seed-bursting. Forces behind man—and woman ...' as a bangled arm shot up, 'behind viruses, superstars and space dust. Call it what you want.'

'No, *you* call it,' cried the woman raising her arm again.

'Go on. Name it, Carruthers,' called Watson dodging in from the back.

'The name!' roared the fat man suddenly, leaning right down over the balustrade and making an ugly, upward movement of his thumb. 'Give the name!'

'Maybe I will,' said Carruthers.

'No maybe's!'

'I will!' yelled Carruthers.

The group on the promenade waited for the next word. At the front the fat man waited, poising himself as though to bear down instantly with all his weight if the answer was not to his liking. Watson, on his toes at the back, waited, staring between motionless heads. The woman had momentarily gripped and silenced her bangles with her left hand. Around these three the rest of the group gradually grew still and as the minutes passed an absolute silence fell. Carruthers gathered himself to speak. From the waist up he stretched and twisted, shaking his shoulders to free himself for the impossible feat, while his stubborn legs stayed fixed. It was just as he raised his head and before he could utter that the wind struck from the north. As the force of it emptied lungs, a sharp, collective gasp went up, followed by an explosive acceleration of sounds. The deck chairs, which had showed only a gentle swell of canvas, began to crack like whips, and a row of billboards against the balustrade clattered onto their faces and went shunting past amongst a mass of flying debris sucked from the tops of litter bins. Across the way the proprietor was slamming down the café windows facing the sea, while above him in his awning a continuous low drumming had started up. There was a snarling swirl of sand and the group at the balustrade turned sideways to a man. Another stinging squall and they had turned their backs to the beach.

For a few seconds the wind dropped. It was quiet except for the sound of one abandoned pail far down the beach, rolling desultorily between two rocks. Then the blast struck again—and with a sharper stuff than sand. Horizontal hail flew past. Balls of ice the size of marbles stotted off the pavement, slid in brilliant pebbled sheets down roofs and ran melting through gutters, piled so thickly they could be heard clashing softly past like crushed metal. At the same time it grew dark, for the harmless little cloud balloons had drifted together into one great mass overhead. One or two, staring through their eyelashes, were now convinced they saw hailstones coming down the size of pingpong balls. Umbrellas, opening up here and there, were quickly snapped in the pelting and a spiky confusion grew as the group started to shove outwards.

'It's stopped!' someone shouted. Everyone paused at that, long enough to look up, long enough to catch a glimpse of blue and observe a three second silence before hail fell again. This time there was no wind. It fell vertically. By now the crowd was moving forward in one body, yet there was an excess of caution which made the attempt look strange. Half-skating, half-shuffling they went, hanging on to one another like beginners testing the rink. Two persons alone showed independence. The fat man was going lightly along on the tips of his toes by the balustrade rail, touching it here and there to steady himself. Watson was far behind the rest. He had turned once to stare back at the beach where Carruthers was still standing. And he yelled to the retreating crowd:

'Hi—wait a minute! You've been swindled—you've been hoaxed! He never said it. Back to the rails, the lot of you, and let him have it! He's given you the slip. He's never going to say it. He's dodged the word! He's dodged God!' No one heard him through the hiss of ice.

Down on the beach Carruthers had let go of his hat and was now squatting in the sand with his arms out like a supplicant, grinning with relief, and letting the hailstones bounce from the open palms of his hands. His hat had blown some distance along the shore, transforming itself as it went. For a while it lay squashed upside down between two rocks, its pulpy, battered crown gummed to the ground, its fronds stirring indolently like a great red and white sea anemone. From there, by a change of wind, it was driven up again and, gaining speed and freedom, went on, now like a bedraggled, reviving bird—half-scuttling, half-flying, towards the sea.

The Clay

Roper had the massive lump of clay delivered inside his front gate. He had never touched the stuff before and as soon as he was alone he gave it a push. It was dense, wet, and unbelievably heavy. He might have been trying to shift a lump of substance on some other planet where gravity was much more powerful than on earth. Nevertheless, he managed to heave it into the close-by garden shed where he decided to leave it for the time being. He could work it there just as well, if not better than inside his house. He remembered that it must be kept wet, so before going to bed he covered the shapeless lump with a piece of soaking cloth and over that put a square of waterproof stuff tied down with tapes to keep the wet in. For a moment it was like embracing some cold, fat shape in a raincoat. But he looked forward to the next few days for he knew the possibilities of bringing the thing to life were endless.

Roper had lately retired from a thriving boxmaking business. In the last years he had removed himself a bit from the actual product for he had sat in a well-appointed, well-insulated container of his own. But from machines in the factory next door he heard the sound of boxes being ejected, second by second, from their hatches and endlessly shuttling along metal rollers, and from his windows throughout the day he'd watch them being piled up and loaded for dispatch in the yards below. Boxes in all sizes were there, from the great metal packing cases, studded with nails, through every kind of wood and cardboard container down to the flimsiest of gift-boxes tricked out in bows and coloured foil. There was a demand for every size and by the time he was due to retire he was a wealthy man. Roper was not married. There were many other things he might have taken up to keep his arteries from hardening, but one day clay had been suggested to him, and clay became his goal. Many times since then he had thought of himself as an aspiring sculptor. Now he meant to prove it.

His lump of clay was roughly spherical and on the second day after its arrival he set to work with a lifesize head in mind. By that time he'd got a heavy stand with a big, central knob to stick the clay on. But he didn't let himself be unduly worried by the tools and techniques of the business. It was to be a slap-happy affair. He gouged oozy lumps off one side and plastered them on another, dug deep into the stuff and plumped it out again. He hummed and whistled as he worked.

'Will you go on leaving it out there in that shed all day and all night?' said Mrs Geer, his housekeeper, when he came in for supper after his first long day on the clay. 'Someone might walk off with it. There's no glass in the windows and the door doesn't even fit.'

'Walk off with that slippery lump!' exclaimed Roper. 'They'd as soon make off with an outsize tub of your dough or a barrowful of wet earth from the garden.'

'Well, they might spoil it for you in the night or in the morning before you're up.'

'Let them try,' said Roper. He slept much better now.

Already all trace of boxes had gone from his dreams. He felt he had escaped his enclosed life and was remodelling another with his two bare hands.

The days went by and Roper worked on and off with the clay in his shed. It intrigued him to work there. It was a travesty of a room, having, as his housekeeper had pointed out, no proper windows and no shutting door, besides which it was cluttered up with gardening tools, old bits of furniture and boxes. In all his working life he had never allowed himself to run out of boxes and there was still a pile of his own brand here—a heavy cardboard type with folding flaps which he kept around in case they should come in useful. Now he kicked them aside to make more room for his work. At first he didn't make much headway. No head emerged from the lump though he dug and smoothed the clay for hours at a time. He pressed it out into a longer shape and tried for a body. No particular form came of that either. He tried for a bowl, a boat, a pylon, a giant pear. No good. Yet he was in high spirits. This was unusual in him and it began to draw comment from passers-by who once in a while stopped to speak to him.

'May I touch it?' asked one girl on her way back from work in a city hardware department.

'Go right ahead,' said Roper. She put her hand through the non-window and touched the clay cautiously with one finger.

'Press harder,' said Roper, 'if you want to get the feel of the stuff.' The girl made a little dent with her forefinger.

'Harder!' Roper cried.

'Help!' she exclaimed. 'Well, all right. I will.' She put both arms through the window and grasped the stuff. As her thumbs sank in and made two soft deep wells she gave

163

a gasp of guilty pleasure. It was years since she had made a mark on anything. Her days were spent amongst metals and plastics—non-stick and non-scratch. She went off down the road, but kept staring back at the shadowy scoops her thumbs had made. Roper kept the scoops. He saw how they could become eye-sockets, so he pressed them deeper, plastered a ridge over them and built up a massive brow above that.

Now at certain peak times of the day there was usually a small group who stopped to watch what Roper was doing. He didn't mind that. Indeed he welcomed it. Some of them were people he'd never seen in his life before. Not all of them were admirers.

'I see you've got a real chinless wonder there,' said one business man who'd watched for a time.

'Yes, it's a highbrow all right,' a woman agreed. 'I never saw a higher one. You could do with something more round that jaw, couldn't you?'

'May I indicate just where?' said the man, dropping his briefcase and pushing in.

'By all means,' said Roper. He was not put out. He enjoyed the staring and arguing round his gate. The man took up a bit of clay, stuck it on one side of the jaw and worked it a bit with his fingers.

'Look out for your cuffs,' said the woman. 'You're not dressed for the job. And by the way, you've made that jaw lopsided. The thing has a gumboil now. Take a bit off there.' She didn't wait for him to do it but reached inside herself, twitched off a piece of clay and patted it round the jaw again till both sides were exactly balanced.

'That's wrong,' said the man. 'It's too symmetrical. What face was ever smooth like that? Not yours for a start.'

'Here—you watch it!' They went off wrangling cheer-

164

fully and others pushed in to take their place.

This was the start of a long free-for-all at Roper's gate. Seeing that he had no objection, many others throughout the day and often in the evening after work helped themselves to the pleasure of manipulating clay. The open windows of the shed, giving on the road, were an invitation. But nobody took away a scrap for himself. The wet cloth was replaced at the end of the day. Cloth, tools, the gate, the shed—everything was left as it had been. Except for the wet lump. It changed continually under a dozen or more different hands. One day a couple of large grey pebbles would fill the eye sockets, giving it a savage glare; on the next specks of gravel gave it a mean and wary look. Sometimes the eyes would be smoothed shut, the lids protuberant, the brow calm as in a death mask. A frowning groove would be dug out between the eyes and deep lines scored above it. Or maybe a pair of outsize ears would be pulled out and the nose lumped into a clown's blob. A few got right away from human head or body. Roper found the clay shaped like a kettle one day. He found a stumpy fish. Once he found a large moist globe with continents and oceans roughly fingermarked round it. He found tilted egg-shapes, cubes and thick clay pancakes. And gradually, after endless changes, the clay would return to a head again—a haggard, battered head looking as if the long fight back from object to human being had been a formidable one. In between times Roper worked at the clay himself, and every new shape gave him new ideas. He changed himself as the summer went on. In his opensided box, exposed not only to the weather but to the judging eyes of the neighbourhood, he now appeared a rather more formidable person—older and tougher, thinner too, as though after his sheltered life he'd let the elements get at him with a vengeance.

Towards the end of the summer Roper was away for over a week. He arrived home late one afternoon and before even putting his bag in the house he went straight to the shed. It was a public holiday—an unusually warm and quiet day, and the place was almost deserted. There were few sounds from the houses. Nobody was on the road. The trees, grown heavier and darker than they had been when he went away, made a shadowy curtain behind the shed and a late, low sunlight struck through its windows. It seemed a stage well set for the benefit of one object and a single spectator. Roper flung down his bag, pushed open the door and went in. Before him on its stand, sunstruck, pale against the gloomy jumble of the shed, was as fine a head in clay as he had ever seen. It was the head of a boy, all the more stunning in contrast to what it had replaced —the bashed turnip shape which had been there when Roper left. The hair was modelled in detail, strand by strand, through the flow of hair from the crown of the head to the turned up ends touching the shoulders. The eyebrows were marked with a feathered curve. The brow was bold. Not for this one were the childish eyes of stone or grit. These slightly bulging eyes had been modelled deep from the clay and looked out at Roper with a mature and challenging expression. Most unexpected of all were the flowers. It was not a garland, as Roper saw when he came close. They had been stuck in separately round the whole head—each one different and all from his own garden. White and yellow roses were here, marigold, geranium, sweet pea and poppy. A bead of fuchsia dangled behind one ear. They were still fresh and Roper automatically looked about him as he stepped from the shed into the garden.

Everything was quiet. Only Mrs Geer had seen him from her window and a few minutes later had joined him outside. Roper had picked up his suitcase again. His face was expressionless. He answered the questions about his holiday with his head turned towards the shed, and when she had finished waited impatiently in silence. At last, following his eyes, she exclaimed:

'Oh—that! That was done—yes, I was flabbergasted myself—by Johnson's boy—you remember him—who used to deliver papers a long time back. Now he's in with the biggest building firm in town. That's him all right. He was here every day for a week and not a person touched it while he was on the job. That head is rather like himself too.'

'Is it indeed?' said Roper.

'And I hope nobody's going to change it for a bit,' she said. 'I've got used to it. I like to see it there. And I like to know it's there. I like to know it's there even when I can't see it.'

Again Roper turned his head to the open door of the shed. The thing changed every moment as the light changed, and in every change it looked good. He gave a short laugh. 'He was here for most of the week? Did he manage to get time off? Most people make do with the time they get. But of course he had plenty of nerve. That I *do* remember.'

'And now he's got plenty of talent it seems.'

Roper was silent. He went inside and touched the blossoms of the head with a finger and smiled. 'Well, that remains to be seen. Oh, this is good all right. But talent is judged by how it goes on.' It was his housekeeper who was now silent, seeing the boxmaker had turned art critic. Privately she wondered if he could sustain the role. Roper went on:

167

'And you let him take flowers?'

'I saw him and didn't stop him.'

'Well of course I don't mind. I suppose he took a new lot every day to keep them fresh. It would be rather odd if everyone did the same. The place would soon be a wilderness. And I see he'd no difficulty at all in finding his way around. Of course he'd had the run of every garden when he was on his papers.'

'Ten different flowers,' Mrs Geer murmured.

'Yes—and some of the best,' said Roper.

'Well, the best needs the best,' she said. Roper said no more about it. In the evening he covered the head none too gently with its damp cloth. He was to be away till the evening of the following day and he planned to leave the clay as it was. 'But, by the way,' he said before he set off next morning, 'you might get in touch with a glazier, will you? Windows without glass are a nonsense. It's only in farce you see such a thing. Freedom's one thing. Pantomime is quite another.'

He was home very late that night. As soon as he got in he went straight to the shed and shone a torch into the darkness. He didn't let the beam find the clay at once. As though fearing a revelation, he first shone the light slowly across the floor, and slowly up the length of the stand and onto the shoulders. He lifted the beam to the head. All was as it had been except that the flowers had been replaced by a wreath of leaves. But not the familiar leaves. He went up close and touched them to make sure. The wreath was made of glossy, dark laurels. Beneath it the skilfully modelled eyes scrutinized Roper's changing expression. The line of the mouth was untouched—still calm and firm, dented at one corner with a faint smile. Roper left the shed quickly, intent on erasing all expression from

168

his face. But his legs were stiff with anger. Mrs Geer was on her way upstairs to bed when he reached the house. With an effort he kept his voice steady. 'Well, Mrs Geer, I see we've got a hero down there now!'

'A hero?' She stared down at him.

'Yes, yes—a young victor!'

'A victor, Mr Roper? Over what?'

'You may well ask. Imagine it. A laurel wreath!'

'I saw that. Well, the flowers were withered, weren't they? Leaves last longer.'

'Oh, but Mrs Geer—laurels! Ordinary leaves wouldn't do. Nothing less than a victor's wreath would do. Have we laurels around here? No, we have not. He had to find them if it meant scouring every garden in the place. The flowers were only a try-out.'

'It's as I've said. Leaves last longer.'

'"Everlasting" is the word you're trying for, Mrs Geer.'

'Is it? I can't stand here all night.'

'Everlasting. Symbol of eternal triumph!'

'Don't excite yourself over a few leaves, Mr Roper. We can remove them in the morning if they bother you.'

'No. Let it stay as it is. I wouldn't dare touch it. And nobody else will either. You wait and see.'

Nobody touched the head, but it drew a crowd of admirers, morning and evening. Sometimes their voices floated up to Roper. Exclamations of admiration and surprise. He waited for jeers. Even a grudging silence would be something. He waited for someone to shove his head inside the shed and shout: 'Enough of that one! Now for my turn!' Nobody took the chance. There were still people around when glaziers arrived to put windows in the shed. They were there when a joiner came to fix the door so that it would shut properly and to fill up cracks between the planks of the roof. At long last it was a proper shed—windproof, waterproof, proof against meddlers or worse. Finally, Roper asked his housekeeper to put up blinds which could be drawn, if need be, to keep out eyes.

'Did you say prying eyes?' said Mrs Geer, astounded at the change in the man.

'I did not. You mustn't impute words to me. I said eyes. Plain eyes. Everyone, however, has a basic right to privacy. Ask anyone in that group down there. Ask them if they've curtains, locks, walls. Am I to be the only one exposed?'

Mrs Geer stared at him, her eyes hostile. Roper put up his own blinds. While doing so he discovered that the joiner had overlooked a hole at the back of the shed—nothing more than an enlarged knot in the wood, but enough for an eyehole. Roper soon fixed it. He put a temporary plug of putty in the hole and set an old chest of drawers against it. And now all was done. He stood one morning in the silence of his sealed shed and realized that he was alone again with the clay head.

Roper touched the head. It was dry and as hard as stone. He put his hands around the nape of the neck to lift off the arrogant leaves and for an instant was staggered by the thought that his touch could as easily have cherished. He flung the wreath into a corner and began to chip away at the head with the first tool that came to hand—a small garden trowel. But this was too light for the job and the clay broke from the head in minute fragments. It would have to be done quicker than that. In the drawer of the chest he found a heavy spanner and a hammer. Under the spanner the clay fell off in lumps and the rest cracked under the hammer into three separate parts. In one part an eye looked up at him in amusement. Roper hammered the bits into a grey powder.

'So that's that,' he said getting up, breathless, from his knees. 'The whole thing was only dust after all.' He swept part of it up easily into a spade and scattered it around the flowerbed nearest the house, far from curious eyes. But in an upper window Mrs Geer stood motionless as though staring at a burial. Roper carried two more shovels from the shed and dug them in deep under the hedge which divided the garden from the road. There was still an enormous quantity of the stuff left in the shed and a breeze blew up as he carried another spadeful out. It blew back over his coat and into his eyes and he saw that some other method would have to be found if he was to finish the job quickly and neatly. For a time he stood in the shed staring, undecided, at the pile of his own cardboard boxes, ivory-smooth, brand-new as they had come from the factory. Reluctantly he opened the lids of two of them and tipped the grey dust and clay fragments inside. Then he closed the boxes up, tied them together with string and carried them round to the back of the house where he dumped them beside the full rubbish bin for the men to carry away next day. Roper brushed the last of the clay dust from his fingers and took a piece of paper and a pencil from his pocket. PLEASE RETURN EMPTY BOXES he wrote in block capitals. This he inserted under the string, then walked briskly round again towards the front door of his house.

Don't Miss It

For the first time in years Stacey had chosen a holiday place on the recommendation of neighbours. On the evening before he left the couple next door looked over the hedge while he was putting out empty milk bottles. 'Listen,' said the man who had once climbed high mountains, 'whatever else you do, don't miss that view I was telling you about. Straight through the village and a mile or two round past the plantation, through the gate on your left and only a step or two up by the ploughed field, and you'll see one of the finest views in the country. You're going to see six mountain peaks and a waterfall from that spot. DON'T MISS IT. Some people come back and say they never saw that view simply because they couldn't be bothered walking a quarter of a mile off the road!'

'And before I forget,' said his wife. 'When you go in the other direction, take the footpath by the river as far as it goes till you come to the broken bridge. Go over it and when you come to the farm with the blue doors strike off across the fields. Right down on your right you'll see the remains of the smallest seventeenth-century castle in the country. Now that *is* easy to miss. Not many people know it. The best time to see it is late evening. If you're lucky and standing in the right place you can see the sun setting through the empty windows. DON'T MISS IT.'

172

'I'll certainly remember that,' said Stacey.

'The thing is that people can be very, very disappointed when they come back and discover they've missed the best view in the country,' said the man.

'I can believe it. I'll not be one of those,' said Stacey.

Next morning after breakfast an older man, Cowan, who lived over the road, came across to tell him once again that it was a very strange thing indeed that he should happen to know every stick and stone of the place Stacey was going to. Brought up within a mile or two of the place. Not only that but his mother had been brought up there and his mother's people from a long way back. In that case Stacey had better not miss the one thing nobody else knew about.

'A little carved head,' said Cowan, 'very high up on the Black Hermit's Tower—so high you'll need your binoculars to see the details. It's no ordinary head. It's in the family. No, I mean it. That head was modelled on my great-great-grandfather, and I've papers to prove it. That's my ancestor stuck right up there on that tower. DON'T MISS IT. Not because it's my family of course. It's the workmanship. It's masterly.'

'It must be good all right,' said Stacey.

'He may not have been important, but he must have been thought goodlooking. Or even just good. But take binoculars. And when you've seen that, you'll want to go right on a mile or so to see the fragment of old wall with the strange inscription.' While they were talking Cowan's grand-daughter had come across, listened for a moment and simply said: 'Ducks.'

'Right,' Stacey said. 'I'll not miss them.'

'Imagine her remembering,' said her grandfather. 'But she's quite right. It's a famous pond of special ducks bred

173

over the years on an estate which will be more or less on your doorstep, as you're staying at Mrs Skene's Guest House. It would be a shame to miss them.'

'I won't,' said Stacey.

'The neck feathers are grey with a very unusual stripe of scarlet.'

'I thought so,' said Stacey. 'I'll not miss that.'

Half an hour before he left, the young couple on his other side looked in with a map and guidebook which they leafed through quickly as Stacey wedged a damp sponge inside a slipper and pressed his suitcase down. 'No, I'll remember that,' he said over his shoulder as he snapped the locks shut. 'That sounds good. A couple of standing-stones in the middle of the high cornfield to the west— no, the east—of the main road.'

'A stone *circle*,' said the girl. 'There are eight of them altogether and they're rather important as a matter of fact —marked on all the maps and with a write-up—a very poor one I may say—in the guidebook.'

'That's interesting,' said Stacey. 'I'll not miss them, though I'll not approach them of course, seeing it's through a cornfield.'

'Oh my goodness—don't worry about that! The farmer doesn't own them,' cried the girl. 'There's a well-marked path across—trodden by centuries of interested persons.'

'I'll be interested,' said Stacey.

'You'll be amazed,' said the young man. They were waving him off now and on his other side, in their window, he saw the middle-aged couple looking out. Grave faces with a touch of disapproval. If you looked long enough you could even imagine a certain sharp envy in their eyes. Stacey could have sworn their lips moved over the phrase:

'He's sure to miss ... he's sure to miss ... the best, the oldest ... the greatest ...'

The weather was warm and clear but the holiday season was over and Stacey had the railway carriage to himself. He was relieved to find himself alone. He was going away for a week only. A good deal of fuss had been made about it, as though an elderly bachelor could hardly be expected to get the most out of a place without the advice of those who had been there before him with sharper eyes, swifter feet and a keener appetite for life. He had been forced to think about the phrase: 'don't miss'. But didn't they know that at his stage he'd missed so many things, was bound to miss so many more that the odd mountain, castle, head, view, wall or bird would now have to take its chance along with the rest? Brave words on the outward journey! But he was not a man of iron will. What would he feel, coming back, if he had missed the lot?

As he unpacked that evening in one of the best bedrooms in Mrs Skene's Guest House, he saw that he had a fine view from the window. Below him was a sheltered garden with a seat where he might sit and read undisturbed in the sunshine to his heart's content. At the evening meal he discovered that the guests, ranging in age from teenagers to pensioners, were all congenial. None of them had heard of the castle and they did not want to hear about it. It was possible that they might look at the rare estate ducks before they left, but again, they might content themselves with the ordinary birds in the nearest pond. They seemed to know in a blinding flash, and with absolute certainty, that they would not want to see the fragment of wall after they had seen the Tower and therefore there was no likelihood that the wall would lead them on to anything else at all. These people were determined to miss a lot. They were even dedicated to it. It was as though Mrs Skene's Guest House had grown up through the years as a centre for all those who wished to avoid seeing what they had been expressly told they ought to see.

Stacey admired the principle but could not follow their example. Always at the back of his mind was a picture of the sharply expectant faces waiting for him back home. He therefore decided to give himself a few days at least of complete freedom before he took on these holiday duties. The days were warm and growing warmer. He had his books. He wrote his letters in the sun. Nothing disturbed his long days in the garden except the husks from a laburnum tree falling on his head and the bees humming in the white and purple clover on the other side of the hedge. He went for walks after supper. His longest walks took him well within striking distance of the castle and even of the Tower. Left to himself he might happily have gone on to find them all. Now it seemed that his way was blocked by a stupendous signpost with the words: DON'T MISS IT. He would begin tomorrow. Not tomorrow but the day after. And now there were three days left. He decided to give them up wholly to sightseeing.

The people at home, in advising him, had strangely enough forgotten one thing about the district. Even the man who knew every stick and stone had not mentioned it. This was the sea. The place was no holiday resort. It was a lonely, unvisited sea, far from the built-up area. It was not what people came for. But it was there—and as powerful in its effects as any other sea. One of these, well-known in the district, was the rising of a white mist called the haar. The haar was different from other mist. It would come after a series of warm days in summer. Rising first

176

as a fine white vapour through which blue sky could still be seen, it would slowly, gradually grow thicker. Even at this stage it might divide to reveal summer again. But only for an instant. An hour later it would have set in. A cold, impenetrable whiteness. Such a mist must not be counted in hours. One day was its shortest term. It had been known to last a week.

The fourth morning of Stacey's holiday was warm and still, but by lunchtime the tree-trunks of a wood overlooking the sea had begun to be wrapped in white. By two o'clock only the highest branches stuck out, like bunches of sticks sailing in a sea of foam. At three no other house in the village was visible from Mrs Skene's windows. Long before supper her garden hedge was gone. The haar had set in and was there to stay. 'We're paying for the warm days,' was the familiar phrase which began to go round.

Stacey went for his usual walk. It intrigued him to take the familiar roads and see only the ground and a yard or two ahead. His own invisibility gave him freedom. The silence sealed him in but also drew him on. This time he even got as far as the Hermit's Tower and was gratified to discover that only the lowest stones round the doorway could be seen. As for the great-great-grandfather he might never have existed. Heights having been washed out, Stacey satisfied himself instead with exploring the depths of the building and climbed—nearly breaking his neck from a loose flagstone—down into the cellars. There was not much of interest. Bits and pieces of old stonework unearthed in the grounds had been stored here along with fragments of urns, tombstones and a broken sundial which would never see the light again. Valuable junk. Too good to discard, not good enough for show. It was a gloomy place. He left quickly, careful to press down the loose flag-

177

stone on his way up again. The Hermit's Tower, as his neighbour said it would, led him on a mile or so to the mound with its fragment of wall and its high, mysterious inscription in Latin. Cowan had made a point of translating it for him: 'WHY GO FURTHER? HAPPINESS, IF IT BE FOUND AT ALL, MUST BE FOUND HERE.' Today the wall could only be located by the quantity of dripping ivy round its base. The plaque with its faint letters had completely vanished. Stacey was cheered and warmed by the discovery. The dogmatic 'must' in the sentence had irritated him when he first heard it. Even now the invisible message 'Why go further?' rankled. He decided to go on.

He was now on the road which led eventually down to the beach—a narrowing, hidden road, for the sea having been written off as a tourist attraction, it was little used. Today it was as far from being a holiday sea as it would ever be. Yet when Stacey came down to the beach he was pleasantly surprised to find it warm and sheltered. There was no wind. The narrow waves were coming in smoothly and quietly from an endless whiteness. Stacey had nothing else to look at but the stones under his feet. They would have had interest for a geologist. Even more for a sculptor. Many of them were large grey pebbles, some barred or ringed with white, and amongst them a few flatter stones with smooth holes worn through. He began to pick them up and threw them as far as he could into the water. Invisible almost as they left his hand, he could judge their distance only by a far-off splash in the surrounding white. He began to make a collection of the rare stones with holes and after a long search sat down to study them. There was one which particularly interested him. It was a large, flattish stone, oval in shape and pierced through at one end by a wide hole. He held it up. It resembled a singing or shouting mouth in a smooth blank face. He discarded the other stones and kept the blank face in his hand as he wandered about the beach again. Occasionally he picked up a stone and compared it with the oval one, but finding nothing to match it in shape and smoothness he at last put it into his raincoat pocket and made for home.

In his room that night he scratched a few lines on the stone with the point of a penknife and was pleased to find them stand out white as an etching against the grey. He went on. He spent a long time marking out two huge eyes and laboriously feathered in the eyebrows above them. These eyes were startling enough but they were no match for the mouth. The shout from this mouth came right through from the back of the head and a long way further out. It was a shout from the back of beyond and it was eerie. He scratched on with his knife and drew a long narrow nose which seemed too calm for this particular face. He added wide nostrils and a broader bridge to the nose. The effect was good. He made it better by a fine criss-crossing of lines on the cheeks to suggest the bone-ridge, and more whiteness in the centre of each eye. Finally he closed his penknife and put the thing flat on his table where it lay staring and shouting. Stacey was proud of his evening's work.

Next morning he found no change in the weather. In a mist denser than ever, he walked along the main road as far as the path which struck off towards the site of the standing stones. He stood on the track trodden by enthusiastic feet, looking out over the cornfield, and was gratified to find that as far as he was concerned there might be a circle of cornstacks up there or even a group of tractors. The whiteness was everywhere. Even the sheeps wool caught in the hedges seemed like the scraps and wisps torn from

179

the mist. He didn't hurry himself. He had been out early and there was time on his way back to make a detour round by the gates of the estate and through to the duck-pond. Here Stacey made a concession. He waited patiently at the pond's edge until one duck had swum close enough for him to bend down and make certain of its colour. Sure enough, the neck was grey with one brilliant streak of red. His sightseeing was over for that day.

He spent his afternoon reading and chatting to the other guests. No one asked where he had gone that morning or why. Mist had muffled curiosity. The lights went on early that evening and the fire was lit in the sitting-room. As for clothes, there had been a swift change from cotton into wool. On the table the cold glass dishes of grapefruit segments had been replaced by broth, the fruit salad and ice-cream by steam pudding and custard. Mrs Skene was obviously used to the 'Happening' from the sea. She knew it would last. Stacey was not so confident. That night he woke for a second, imagining, with sinking heart, that he had glimpsed a shred of moon in the wardrobe mirror.

It was a false alarm. Next day was as thick as ever. After lunch he walked some distance out of the village and then, with careful steps, took the river footpath for a mile or so before turning to look in the direction his neighbours had advised. As he expected, the castle was blotted out. In the hollow place where the ruin stood, mist had gathered as though trapped. This castle could be seen, if you knew where to look as simply a clot of mist rather denser than the rest of the surrounding whiteness. Stacey stood for a while satisfying himself that there could be no possible chance of seeing the sun setting through its windows either that night or the night after. It was the last day of his holiday. He returned to the house happy, as though he'd seen every sight in the book.

On the following day he was not due to leave till mid-afternoon. He did his usual hour's reading in the morning. The rest of the time he spent on his stone. For a while he sat with it in the palm of his hand, turning it about in light and shade, setting it up and laying it flat. Then, with great care, he scored a few lines across the forehead and slowly drew out the corner of each eye into a ray of fine lines. He did nothing to the mouth. The mouth and its shout were fixed forever. But the head was older. It seemed his own age now, but a good deal tougher. Stacey decided the shout was a mocking one. He got his things together and just before he was due to leave he made one more outing. He paid a second visit to the Hermit's Tower.

Five miles inland the mist began to thin out. From the train Stacey saw it moving close to the window in long shreds which gradually divided to give glimpses of great clouds of mist rolling off the fields and dissolving up into a clear blue sky. A mile or two further, and there were only a few wisps caught in the trees and some patches here and there in the hollows between bright green hills. He arrived back early on a brilliant evening. The station-master was sympathetic about his tale of haar. Since he left not a day had passed but had been as fine and clear as this one. For at least an hour after he got home Stacey was undisturbed. He opened his mail, unpacked and pottered about the house. In the bin he found a week-old loaf which made toast better than any he'd had in the Guest House. At seven, with soup simmering in a pan, he went into the garden to pick parsley. His arrival had not gone unnoticed. His appearance outside was as good as an invitation.

'Yes, yes,' said Stacey to the neighbours who were coming in from his right. 'A splendid week—every minute of it—never a week went so quickly as this one. The weather? No, it was *not* perfect.' On his left the middle-aged couple were now looking over the hedge enquiringly.

'Yes, every minute of it,' said Stacey. 'The weather changed, of course. But in spite of those last three days I managed to get around.'

'So you got around and saw things?' said the left-hand wife.'

'No. I said I got around,' Stacey said, rapidly picking parsley from the border below the hedge. 'I saw nothing.'

'But you did, of course, see the castle—the view of the six peaks and the waterfall?' Their eyes flashed. The small top twigs of the hedge snapped as they leaned across.

'I saw nothing,' said Stacey. He explained as best he could the mist and its density, while behind him, inside his gate, the others waited.

'In my experience,' now came the voice of his younger neighbour, 'no one has *ever* been to that district and missed the stone circle!' He and his wife were moving quickly up the garden path.

'It's just not possible!' his wife agreed.

'Then I may be the first,' said Stacey. '*I* have missed it. I have made it possible.' The moment of incredulous silence was almost immediately broken by the arrival of the man from across the road.

'Been on the look-out for you all day!' he exclaimed, leaning over the gate. 'Knew you'd be coming either on the ten o'clock or the three o'clock ... wanted to hear all about it while it was still fresh and clear in your mind.'

'A great week,' said Stacey. 'But clear? Most of the time I couldn't see my own hand in front of my face!'

His opposite neighbour ignored this. '... Wanted to hear

how the great-great-grandfather's weathering these days. How's he doing all alone up there on his tower? Notice the curious curl of his beard? Those gay little tassels on his cap?'

Under the scrutiny of five pairs of sharp eyes Stacey again explained his haar. It was hard to conjure it up for them out of the brilliant evening light. They were still staring at Stacey as though to get at him through some mythical mist where he might still be hiding. It was the man from across the road who at last spoke for them.

'So you missed everything!' he cried. A silence of judgment filled the garden.

'Not *everything*,' said Stacey, blowing a little dust from his parsley. 'You never told me about the other head in the tower.'

'There is no *other* head!' said the teacher, and the gate rattled.

'Not on the tower itself. I mean the head under the flagstone on the cellar steps. The shouting head—the singing head—whatever it's called. You've never seen it! But surely one of you—? Never even *heard* of it! No one who really knows the place could possibly miss it. No. Don't ask me the where and the when and the why. Because I can't tell you. Nobody knows. But one of these days, no doubt, it'll disappear into some museum or other at the back of beyond and that'll be that. DON'T MISS IT!' He smiled at them and turned away. 'You'll excuse me now. I have some soup ready. Oh, and the duck,' Stacey called over his shoulder. 'That was another thing. Tell your grand-daughter I saw the red streak of the duck!' He waved, stepped inside, and rather quietly—in order not to disturb the neighbours more than seemed to him strictly necessary—he closed the door of his house.

A Polite Man

One day, coming up towards the cruellest peak of a noon rush-hour in the city, a middle-aged man was passing through the doorway of a large department store on his way to buy a suitcase. He was struck suddenly by some memory from the past—or rather, it was an instinct battered down by years of shoving and pushing with the rest, and almost muffled under the continuous swish of heavy doors swinging back in outraged faces. This instinct to show some politeness to his fellow-men, battered but not yet dead, suddenly revived in him and sprang to life upon his lips in a convulsive grimace of civility. As he pushed against the heavy door he stopped dead, and by exerting a good deal of backward pressure on his right arm, he managed to hold it open for the person coming behind.

He knew no reason why he should do such a thing at that particular moment. He had not even looked behind to see who was coming. It turned out, however, to be a well-dressed young man carrying a parcel under one arm and a rolled umbrella hooked over his wrist. This man looked surprised and pleased that the door should be held open for him and as he passed through he directed a brilliant smile straight into the other's eyes. Then he went on and was soon lost to sight within the depths of the shop. The older man remained where he was, holding the door and looking after him, hardly aware that half a dozen other persons had passed through and were already going about their business up and down the long counters.

He was now holding the door with only the tips of his fingers, ready to plunge forward whenever it was taken from him. But now a regular stream of people were coming from behind and squeezing by without touching the door with their hands. Some of them—perhaps by holding their breath—managed to shrink themselves into such a shape that while they were going through no bit of them came into contact with door or man. Even the dogs went cringingly through. It was a feat which demanded great muscular control and determination, and for a while the man was forced to give up all thought of his own escape. Instead, he stood well to one side behind the door, still gripping its edge tightly with one hand. From time to time the rushing stream of persons diminished. One or two would go by more slowly and it would seem as though they were about to take the door from him. But after touching it as though simply testing the grain of wood, or lightly pressing with the fingertips like ballet-dancers during an awkward turn, they would pass through. Occasionally someone would turn to him to give a smile or a nod. One or two wished him good morning, and a few remarked on the coldness of the day outside.

It was cold enough where he stood. The puffs of warm air from the shop were no match for the freezing draught which blew steadily in from the street. All the same, he still had some care for his own comfort and he was amused when it suddenly struck him that there had been no need to grip the heavy door so hard. Just below his fingers was a large brass handle into which he could comfortably put his whole hand. When he pulled on this, leaning well back on his heels, he found it possible to rest his back and even his legs for several minutes at a time. He noticed, too, that by placing his hand in this new and more natural position he had also affected the attitude of the customers towards him. On the whole, they seemed glad to see him there. They no longer shrunk themselves into such a meagre shape. Their movements were less constricted and they were freer with smiles and words.

His position at the door was accepted, however, with one reservation. There was obviously something wrong with his appearance—something puzzling and unsatisfactory. Those who did glance at him would drop their eyes swiftly to the buttons of his overcoat, raise them again to his brow and drop them once more down to the turn-ups of his trousers. The man at the door began to feel uncomfortable himself. He decided that in spite of the cold he would feel better if he were to remove his soft hat. Twenty minutes later, he reluctantly unbuttoned his brown tweed overcoat and folded it carefully over a nearby chair. There was still a good deal that was inadequate about him—he realized that—but at the same time he felt more secure in his position, whatever it might turn out to be.

The lunch hour had come and gone. By now, all those who had passed him earlier, on their way in, had long ago emerged with their purchases and disappeared again into the outside world. Long ago the young man with the umbrella had gone by, this time showing neither surprise nor pleasure at the door held open for him. The older man who had a smile ready, as friendly as the one he had received earlier, was forced to deflect it towards his own image mirrored in the thick glass behind which he stood. At the same time he felt the cold worse than ever.

There were certain things, however, which made up for

the difficulties and disappointments he had experienced during the last few hours. By far the most important of these was the discovery of a small brass latch fixed to the floor behind the door, close to his feet. It meant, in fact, that now even the labour-saving brass handle was not necessary. To keep the door permanently open he had only to draw it right back until he heard the cunning little click indicating that it had been secured by the latch. He could then stand by with his hands perfectly free.

Once again, this change affected his relations with the people going in and out. The freedom of his hands had made him more available in other ways and from now on he was constantly questioned as to the whereabouts of different departments and even asked for the exact location of a wide variety of objects, ranging from kettles and corsets up to church organs and whole suites of drawing-room furniture. And he was now able to answer these enquiries by swinging his arms around, or bending sideways, backwards and forwards, in an effort to direct people up and down flights of stairs or along the corridors which led to the lifts. He welcomed this change. He was still a fixture, but a movable one, like those toys which at first sight appear able only to nod gently, but contain strong springs and can be screwed far round in every direction, even bending forward with their heads between their feet without losing balance.

But as the day wore on he began to feel more and more uneasy. By standing on this small patch of floor he had cut himself off from the outside world without effectively joining himself to the one inside. Moreover, he was now aware that his deficiency, whatever it was, had become a serious drawback. For however quickly he pointed and nodded and swung himself backwards and forwards from heel to toe, it was obvious that few people placed any confidence in him. Some of those who asked to be directed went so far as to put the exact same question to someone else before they had taken a couple of steps from the door and while well within earshot.

It was at this point in the day he suddenly remembered —as though looking far back into another existence—that he had entered this place with the definite intention to buy. But what had he come in for? Hard as he tried to place this object, something prevented him from defining it. This much he knew. It had about it the quality of escape. It suggested in various subtle and insidious ways connected with its opening and shutting, the gay click and snap of its fastenings, that there were better places he could be standing than on this particular spot by a permanently open door. It even gave rise to the outrageously irresponsible notion that not only the solid earth, but also the air and the sea were awaiting him—that if he were tempted to leave this place even for an instant he could plunge headlong into a sparkling, dizzying element where clouds, stars and fishes shone, where fruited palmtrees and thick-petalled flowers waved and beckoned.

But he dispelled these thoughts and with them threw away forever the unlikely notion that his original purpose had been to come here for a mere box of some kind. At the same time his face became more pinched and severe, as though he had just thought of something which did this shop a great discredit. Now, with an immense effort, he stepped from his place behind the door and moved rigidly forward through the crowd in search of some person in authority. As he moved further and further in, he was aware how vulnerable he had become, how nakedly exposed even to the most casual glance.

188

But he now knew beyond any doubt what it was he had come here for, and lifting his eyes to the face of the manager who loomed enquiringly over him, he said in a voice, quiet, yet bitterly reproachful:

'Sir, I have been on the job since morning. I have waited patiently all day—through the lunch-hour and through the tea-breaks. Now it is nearly closing-time, and still no sign of it. There is nothing for it but to bring the matter to your personal attention. Sir, I must beg you—kindly let me have my uniform.'

The Bookstall

Early one winter evening, a man called Molson was leaning against the bookstall of a crowded platform waiting for the home-bound train. He was a busy man, proud to account for every instant of a prominent official's day. It was even his boast that these moments in the station, and the half-hour's journey following, were the only times he was completely free. Yet he was an optimist. Years of commuting had not absolutely killed his feelings for the place—a belief, though he'd never lived up to it, that at every railway junction came the promise of escape from routine. He saw the glass rather than the iron in his surroundings. But there was a pessimist's view of stations. Its outlook was all iron—unbending and uncompromisingly black. Molson acknowledged it—he even felt slight twinges of it in his bones as he waited tonight—but he could never agree with it.

A full train had just drawn out. It was some time before the next was due. '*That* was a heavy one,' said the girl behind the bookstall, leaning out towards him over ranks of paperbacks. Her job made her well-known to everyone—though being looked at was another matter, competing as she was with her customers' constant anxiety with time. But even more than with the clock, she had to compete with the faces and figures on book-covers. A swirling pattern of girls lay before her—nurses, witches and schoolgirls, nuns, queens, spies and housewives, some holding knives and guns to men's heads, and some—raped by gorillas, bitten by vampires, worried by werewolves—were swooning back upon beds and hammocks, upon operating-tables and altars, and some into pits and graves or into whirlpools, strangled by their own hair.

'I said—a heavy *train* tonight,' the girl repeated, leaning still further out as though she would grasp Molson by the lapel. Glossy, butter-blonde hair swung across the books as she turned her head this way and that to attend to paper-grabbers on either side of her. Her expression was not sympathetic.

'Yes, indeed—a very busy train.' Molson automatically looked behind her to see if the other woman was around. He imagined her as the motherly type.

'Mrs Woodlock is not back from her tea,' said the girl following his glance. Something sardonic in her tone made him turn to the platform again. It had suddenly grown quiet—that rare interval when officials can be heard chatting in the booking-office and even, tonight, the swish of an outsize platform brush cleaning up dust and old tickets on the other side of the line.

'Where in the world can they be rushing to—morning, noon and night?' said the girl standing back with her arms folded. Startled, Molson turned round. 'Where can who ...?'

'All those people—as though their lives depended on it, for heaven's sake!'

It crossed Molson's mind that talk along such lines could lead to difficulty. 'Well, probably their lives *do* depend on it,' he said. 'For one thing they are going back and forth to their work.'

'And for another?'

'What did you say?'

'What are the other things?'

Molson silently folded his papers and put them under his arm as though he must very soon be moving off himself. He held the view that the business of bookstall women, in the racket of stations, was to be both static and silent. But the girl, as though instantly snatching this thought, said: 'Oh, *we* stay put of course. There's plenty of chance to watch. But I was asking—what are all the other things people do in your opinion?'

'The other things? Well, that's putting it wide enough, isn't it? People visit their friends and relatives, I suppose. But mainly there's all the business in and around the jobs —organizing, contacting, interviewing ... well, the thing is endless. To put it simply—people go to meetings.'

'People like yourself?'

'I admit I *am* a very busy man.'

'Important?'

Oh, the nerve of the round, blue eyes. 'No, busy,' he said sharply. 'I have commitments—responsibilities.' In the heavy silence that followed he actually heard birds twittering and flapping around the arches of the roof.

'They come in through the broken panes this time every evening, regular as clockwork,' said the girl.

'Well, they certainly don't follow the clockwork in *this* station. There's that clock stopped—and that, and that!' He jabbed an umbrella in their direction.

'Mrs Woodlock says that sometimes, just before a train's due, every one of them stops whistling.'

'Mrs Woodlock?'

'We do have names. My name's Estelle. Mrs Woodlock's

no fool. She's been all over the world of course. But not in the usual way.'

'Not in the usual way?' asked Molson. Did the woman have wings?

'Oh no. Years ago she got in with this top trombonist. She followed him in bands up and down the country and across Europe more times than she can count. And for more years. He could put his hand to anything—that one. Bright wasn't the word.'

Molson stared about him as though vainly searching for something to take the shine off the man. Only one wan thing occurred to him. 'And did he ever marry her?' he said at last.

And now, as though conjured up from the shadowy depths of the stall, Mrs Woodlock herself appeared behind Estelle's shoulder. A pair of black eyes in a heavy white face studied him. Dense, wavy hair held up by jewelled combs made her head seem massive, and now and then, as she pushed one further in, there came a glitter as though an icicle had been crushed, unmelted, to her scalp.

'We've been talking about how busy everybody is these days,' said Estelle.

'Well, we've certainly an opportunity to see it here,' said Mrs Woodlock, 'but of course I don't equate rushing around with work. We're busy enough ourselves. But we simply stand all day.'

'As you know by your legs,' said the girl.

'As I certainly know by my legs,' Mrs Woodlock agreed. The dark eyes and the blue watched him.

'I suppose someone has to organize the world's affairs— someone must try to keep things straight,' said Molson, his glance falling on dishevelled figures fleeing from vampires.

'This gentleman tells me he's busy enough anyway,' said Estelle. 'He has these endless meetings.'

'Whom does he meet?' asked Mrs Woodlock with a smile. 'A meeting can be a very pleasant thing. I see endless meetings here on this very platform. Some of them look as if they might turn out to be very agreeable indeed.'

'This is the other kind—around tables,' said the girl.

'Tables are all right,' said Mrs Woodlock.

'These are those polished tabletops. No food,' said Estelle.

'Oh those! Well, there's not much pleasure to be had in that. Just paper, pencils and glasses of water. Oh yes, I've had a sight of those meetings and it's a very dismal business indeed!'

Molson had begun to show little relish for this discussion of himself as a busy man. Oh, to get onto some other tack— present himself as an adventurer, a reckless wanderer such as the trombonist must have been! Instead, by cruel force of habit, he found himself taking the diary from his inside pocket. With his back to the bookstall he flicked quickly through it. These pages were black with engagements. There were names, addresses, times, underlinings in black and red, arrows pointing down to future dates and back to past ones. Certain places and persons stood out where the ballpoint had instinctively thickened itself upon them. Fainter lines marked dates of less importance. Even the crossings-out varied from the bold, impatient stroke to the narrow line. There appeared to be a sign-language here decipherable only by the dedicated diarist. 'Not many blanks *there*!' came Mrs Woodlock's voice from behind him. Whatever the language was, it interested the two women. They were bending forward over the stall. Both were smiling. But he had the feeling it was their own secrets which amused them. Their faces, as they leaned towards him, came into shadow, but the stall lights shone down directly and theatrically on top of the blonde and the black head. This was their stage. Molson had no inkling what the entertainment was about.

'No, there are *not* many blanks,' he said. 'Year after year my diaries get filled up. There's not much I can do about that, I'm afraid.'

'A diary!' exclaimed Estelle. 'Of course we sell plenty of diaries ourselves at New Year. It's always struck me as a very funny name to give them. I'd always thought of a diary as a day-to-day account of exciting events. Did it strike you like that, Mrs Woodlock?'

'Yes,' said Mrs Woodlock. 'A daily write-up of happenings is my idea of a diary. As a matter of fact Johnson kept a diary for many years—a real diary, you understand. But then of course he did have something to record. There weren't many countries he hadn't set foot in. He knew the lot. As for people—he met all sorts and he was a match for all sorts. Of course trombones weren't the whole of it, by any means. He was a first-rate chess player, an excellent cook, and I'd say he was a bit of a magician too. More than a bit. A hypnotist. You could almost say he made them see white where there was black.'

In the pause following Molson felt an unpleasant frisson of nerves. 'But not white to black, I hope,' he said.

'Oh no. Johnson was a good man. He didn't play malicious tricks—even when people deserved them. But he was clever all right. Once he found this gigantic advert on the hoarding outside a hall he was to play in. Cigarettes it was—cigarettes and the fantastic joy and peace of lighting up beside a river with nothing but a pack of hounds to keep you company. Well, Johnson took exception to it, a love to hatred turned you might say. He'd been a wheezy man once, you see, a very wheezy man before he broke the habit. It very nearly cost him his job. Anyway, there he was staring at this thing till quite a crowd came up to see for themselves. "Why must they always keep this great blank placard on the wall," he kept saying, "when so many good things could do with a bit of advertising? Me, for a start. Doesn't that waste of space offend you? Doesn't that great white glare hurt your eyes?" And, believe it or not, there were always two or three who saw a blank and nothing but a blank. I'm telling you God's truth. He had the power and some fell under. Didn't I say he could make black white?'

Molson put up a hand to loosen his collar, but he managed to smile, murmuring: 'There must be some gullible people around.'

'Oh, very likely,' replied Mrs Woodlock with ominous restraint. A red spot had appeared on one cheek and her eyes flashed.

'Gullible!' exclaimed Estelle. 'Bamboozled by a cigarette the size of a tree-trunk and a puff of smoke like a mushroom cloud! There's "gullible" if you like!'

'At any rate he taught me a thing or two that's helped me no end in a tough, ungrateful life,' said Mrs Woodlock, still speaking with straight lips. 'Call them tricks if you like.'

'No, no, of course not,' Molson said quickly. Very high up, somewhere amongst the broken panes and the birds, he heard rain falling, and a wind was finding its way under old, bolted doors and up abandoned stairways. Lights only emphasized the darkness of pillars and girders. The whole place lay under a coating of black. Why couldn't they scrub off this gloom as they did with other buildings?

Estelle, who'd been silent for some time watching Molson, leant forward: 'No amount of cleaning would help,' she said. 'Everything's iron here. Painting might do it. But who'd spend money?'

This time Molson took care that his nerves should not be visible in his face, but his limbs looked eager to be away. Even his arms made ineffectual gestures towards the end of the platform as though signalling his train to emerge suddenly from the tunnel and deliver him. But this was not to be.

'I don't think it's coming yet. I think it will be very late tonight.' Even as Mrs Woodlock uttered these words the booming announcement of its lateness filled the station. 'How unpleasant—having to hang around here,' she said with biting amiability. There was nothing to keep him, yet Molson still leaned against the bookstall as though pasted on by his pocket.

'Have you got all the papers you want?' Mrs Woodlock went on. 'A busy man has to keep up with things, hasn't he? Periodicals?' Molson stretched over and picked up a couple of weeklies.

'Books?' Mrs Woodlock persisted.

'They are not exactly my kind.'

'Oh, you'd be surprised,' said Mrs Woodlock with a smile, not explaining if the surprise was in the books or the people who bought them.

Molson had an armful of newsprint now—enough for the longest journey. It made him no more popular at the bookstall. He had long come to the conclusion that this pair had an ingrained hatred of the papers they were handing out.

'You've got a nice pile to get through before the night's out,' said Estelle. 'Yes, a man *does* need to keep himself informed.'

197

'Not every man,' said Mrs Woodlock. 'I must say Johnson was different. That's to say he was well-informed all right. Prodigiously. But he didn't rely *only* on the print. Oh goodness no! Most of his information he got by moving round the world. Using his wits. Wits, Estelle—that's what we miss these days. Information to the eyeballs, facts at the fingertips—oh dear, yes—but where are the wits?'

Molson was silent, his head bent over the papers on the stall, as if intent on drawing the very heart and guts from the world's news.

'But don't let us disturb you,' said Mrs Woodlock. 'For us it's different. Any chance for a chat in a long day. But we're used to looking at tops of heads; I am quite an expert myself. Believe me, it would never occur to us to try and compete with print.'

The platform was now filling up again and Molson felt some return of optimism—only a scrap, but enough to get him on the move again.

'. . . Signalled at last,' he said firmly.

'Have a good journey,' said Estelle. 'Anyway, good or not, you've got plenty to occupy you.'

'Yes, that'll keep you going,' echoed Mrs Woodlock. 'Never a dull moment—and I hope you've good eyes.' Estelle and Mrs Woodlock smiled and smiled at him, but only with their mouths. The black and the blue eyes were boring into his with remarkable intensity.

'Goodnight, Mrs Woodlock ... goodnight, Estelle,' said Molson, careful to get the names across and to pronounce them well.

'Goodnight,' said Mrs Woodlock, 'but I don't think we've had the pleasure ...' There was a grimness about this familiar phrase—something almost approaching a threat. Molson was about to give his own name when he was engulfed by a group who had emerged from the buffet and were hurling themselves at the bookstall for last-minute buying. He had the sensation of falling back as he started to speak. From a distance he tried to utter his name again, and again shouts drowned the sound. There was no knowing whether it came out as cry or whisper, or whether he had perhaps not opened his mouth at all. Molson suffered a momentary and appalling loss of identity. But with the arrival of his train his attention turned to finding a seat. It was only when he was seated and had time to wipe the steam from his window that he looked towards the book-stall. He had a flashing glimpse of Mrs Woodlock and Estelle between the heads and shoulders of bystanders. To say they were laughing was an understatement. Molson marvelled that the jokes of late commuters could produce such mirth.

The train was full, but it was fast with one stop only where, twenty minutes later, his compartment emptied, leaving one other man. Usually at this point in the journey Molson would start on his papers. But not tonight. Tonight he sat with one hand on them, waiting for his mind to settle. As black fields, lines of street-lights, factories, bridges and rivers flashed past, so his imagination flew from one scene to another over the past week. He saw small committee-rooms fitted like Chinese puzzles inside large committee-rooms, and the long, windowless corridors which stretched ahead through a series of revolving doors. He saw his trays of letters, trays of rubber stamps, trays of coffee-cups. He saw halls of typewriters, silent under their night covers. In the dark landscape, between sheep and cows, telephones gleamed, and filing-cabinets. Huge, black-lettered office calendars slid by across clumps of trees. In front of all these, brighter and more ravaged, floated his own face. Molson turned his head away quickly and nodded to the man in the opposite corner—known to him by sight though not by name. They were travelling companions, meeting occasionally on platforms and in waiting-rooms. They shared grievances.

'Later every day!' the man exclaimed. He stared at his watch, sighed, and fixed his eyes on the space above Molson's head. 'Ideal holiday, is it?' he said at last. '... Acres of bog and a crumbling castle! No thanks—not for me.' Molson sat tight as though chary of a crick in the neck. The man's eyes wandered to a space on the other side. 'Now *that*'s more like it. If you can rely on that golden sand and the purple sky. And in my experience of adverts it's a very big "if".'

Still Molson made no attempt to verify the colours. Instead, he quickly picked up the top paper on his pile and looked down the front page pictures. Statesmen stared out at him, honest-eyed to an alarming degree. He turned over to the back and read the fortunes of footballers and found himself going methodically down the list of names chosen for some unknown swimming team. After some minutes, Molson turned to the middle pages—and his heart jerked in his chest as though shaken by derailment. He turned to others. Between back and front every page was empty—blank and dingy as unprinted cotton. Molson raised the paper to hide his face. Once in a while, he told himself, it was bound to happen. Some freak paper amongst hundreds of thousands would get through. Stealthily, scarcely rustling it, he folded it and laid it down. He picked another—an evening paper—and held it for a time, still folded, in both hands, as though reassuring himself of its proper weight of black print, then swiftly opened it in the middle. These pages—blank from top to bottom—

brought ice patches to his cheeks. This time he'd not been careful to hide his face.

'Look here, you're not cold, are you?' came the voice from the other corner. 'Just a minute. I believe there's a window open.' He got to his feet and Molson heard him some way along the corridor pushing a window up, saw him come in again, careful to slide the compartment door tightly behind him. Molson thanked him briefly, folded his paper again and placed it on top of the other. The man was still watching. 'There *is* flu about,' he said, 'and then of course it does none of us any good—all that hanging about on the platform.'

Molson agreed it had done him no good at all. He sat back again and tried to take a grip on himself. What had happened? Nothing had happened—nothing except that the bookstall women between the two of them had managed to give him a set of dud papers. That was the beginning and end of it. A poor trick. Why, then, this appalling loss of nerve?

The train was making up for lost time. Small stations flashed past in a single chain of blue and yellow light. Tunnels were reduced to the momentary lowered note. Molson was glad of the speed. For a time the sensation seemed to smooth out thought. Yet in spite of this, an increasing unease came over him as he saw in the distance the lights of one of the larger stations. He sat forward on the edge of his seat and looked out. The train was almost at the station and reducing speed slightly as it approached. And now, for a few seconds, Molson was staring into the empty station, staring with such anxiety in his eyes that a solitary porter on the platform craned his neck to get a further sight inside the carriage as it went past. Molson himself had the flashing impression of familiar lights and stairways, walls and sign-boards—then they were out again into the countryside. But he was still sitting forward. All was not right with the station back there. It was not something he cared to name. What else, he decided, but an illusion from speed and darkness—the flicker of white spaces where the posters should be, that great, blank sign-board without a name? It was far behind him now. Molson settled back into his corner, but before three minutes had gone by, cautiously, as though lifting a baited trap, he took up one of the weekly journals. Its cover had the familiar, cheerful layout in black and red. One hand pressed to his lips, he flicked the page over. There was empty paper inside. Molson dropped it on his knee and grabbed up the second weekly—cheerful again in black and green. Every square inch between front page and back—hopelessly blank! Molson let them slide down onto the pile beside him.

'... Only if you're absolutely finished with them ...' the voice came from the other corner.

'Take them—take them!' Getting to his feet Molson lifted the wad of papers in both hands and let them drop with a thud on the seat opposite. The other's good nature faded a little. 'Thanks,' he said, 'but I'll hardly get through that lot, will I? Not unless we've more than the usual hold-ups.' He got no answer. Molson was staring through the window on his own side as though life depended on it. Yet nothing outside held him rigid. He was staring at the reflection of the man in the opposite corner. Molson watched as he took up the evening paper, saw him run his eye down the front page, and waited an age while he turned it. His expression didn't change. He spent a long time on this page and on the one after it. Certain bits he read more intently, holding the sheet close to his face.

'A very peculiar paper tonight, I think you'll admit,' said Molson. His rigid face cracked in a smile.

'No different from any other night to my mind,' said the other, 'except for that chap drowning himself first soak off in his solid gold bathtub. Then of course there's the woman helping the police with the hand and the three ears in the laundry bag. Three! That certainly makes you think.' Another age passed before he picked up the second paper. 'The odd thing is,' he said at last, 'the daily doesn't say a word about either of them. I've been through it from end to end—not a word! No gold bathtub. No ears. Whether or not the pound's had a good day—oh yes. There's always plenty on that subject. Do they ever worry about what kind of day we've had. *You're* not looking any too great. Anyway, thanks ...' He was about to hand back the papers when Molson leant over and pushed his arm back.

'Wait!' he said. 'Did you look at those weeklies?' His peremptory tone made the other man gape. 'I gave you the lot, didn't I? Read the lot!'

The other's annoyance increased dramatically. 'Here— take them! Did I ask to have the whole damn load dumped on me?' He took the pile of papers, delivered them with a thump to the other seat and retired into his corner. After some minutes he took an engagement diary from his pocket and absorbed himself in it.

Molson stared across at him, struck by a chilling thought. He began searching for his own diary—through every pocket of his overcoat, in the zipped side-flaps of his brief-case. The search was pointless. The book, he knew, was where it always was and always would be, year after year— in the left-hand inner pocket of his jacket. He dreaded finding it. Amongst the remembered voices of that day one rose clear above the rest: 'Not many blanks *there*!' Mrs Woodlock had exclaimed on sight of the diary. With what venomous sarcasm she had uttered it!

Molson drew out the flat, green book and laid it on his knee. For a long time he stared at it, willing its contents to be intact. The diary was still warm from being close to his chest. It was a heart of a kind—reliable and exact. No matter if each year there was a change of heart. In essence it was always the same. Molson opened the first page, and his heart leapt. His name, his address, his phone number, his car number—all there, thank God! On the second page and third—Driving Licence, TV Licence, Credit Card and Passport Number, Bank Book and Blood Group, Date of Birth and Glove Size. He was not totally annihilated. Still, with fearful caution he turned other pages. It was as it had always been—the names in black and red, underlinings and circlings, scribbled letters and block letters. Page after page he turned. He found no gap. His timetable stood firm and clear on all its lines between the red dates.

'Not a blank in the whole book—see for yourself!' cried Molson to the man in the corner and he waved the diary in the air. 'Crammed to the covers. Not a space, not a gap, not a chink!'

But the other was still smarting from their last exchange. 'And what about it?' he replied. 'Couldn't I say exactly the same myself? Amn't I up to the neck in it this year, next year and well on into the next again? If it comes to that I could fill up a three-year diary any day you wanted it. No trouble at all. Oh no, don't talk to me about blanks!'

Molson wasn't listening. He was trying to crush a massive wad of papers into the narrow space under the seat. He was not absolutely successful. A corner of one paper still protruded, but he put his heel on it. Unbelievable vacancies haunted his mind, but his own cosmos was safe. He took out his pen and double-lined certain dates in his diary. His stroke was tremulous to begin with but it gained firmness as he went on. Once in a while he paused to sharpen up an asterisk star, and here and there where the nebulous circles had grown faint, thickened them with a darker line.

The Last Word

Very early in life Pirie decided that the world owed him a lot and that never, for as long as he might live, could the debt be made up. But he could still take back something for himself. It was natural for him as a child to take everything that moved under his hand. He went after fluff-balls and the twists of paper that fell from pockets. He chased tickets and picked up the feathers dropped by birds. He was like a bird himself. His bead-green eyes scanned the ground as through a magnifying lens. Later he interested himself in scatterings of coins, notes and cigarettes. He was no different in this from any other. But as he grew older he lifted his head from the ground and saw things ready for the taking on shelves and ledges. He hardly needed a conjurer's skill to dip into the fruit baskets of small shops or remove four or five from a row of identical leeks. The world owed him melons as well as plums. It owed him serving-plates as well as ashtrays. But the small things were easiest to stow.

When he was grown and on a level with others his eyes never melted with theirs. His parents seemed to him as smugly respectable as the two white china figures on either side of their wedding-day clock which had been allowed to run slow ever since. Two brothers and a sister had made themselves ridiculous, in his eyes, by passively accepting over the years the uniforms, the wages, the dead-ends of their various jobs. He despised them for this. He was intelligent himself, good both with head and hands. But he had a dread of the static life. Instead he went in and out of an endless variety of trades, helping himself as he left to tools and clocks, towels, lamps and paperweights. He was on his way to becoming a petty thief, yet the name didn't suit him. He had begun to have judgment. He seldom picked an ugly thing though he took useless ones. Nor was it certain he'd be thrown into ecstasy even if his foot had accidentally grated on a diamond. This might have seemed crude and obvious as a free gift. It would heave meant fate had softened towards him and he had no use for softness.

But he had to have money. He'd built up a car-cleaning business with another man. He'd assembled furniture, assisted a firm of auctioneers and tried juggling dishes in restaurant-cars between London and Edinburgh. But at the same time his liftings became more ambitious. He was no smasher or slasher. He had grown excessively reserved and in certain ways almost as respectable as his family had been. Gradually the pilfering grew into a fine art. To take jobs for money was one thing. This was something else. Nowadays the world didn't owe him anything or everything. It owed him the best, the unusual, the hard-to-get. There were never many things in his room at one time for he was never satisfied. He discarded endlessly, letting go of one prize only to pick a better. A model ship changed places with binoculars which were replaced, after a week or two, by a chessboard, a chunk of agate, a stuffed heron with toes embedded in blue rock. The best was to be had if only he could lay hands on it. When it was found he was willing to pay and pay high, for he was after pearls of price. Meantime, he helped himself.

Pirie saw himself as quick, cool and deliberate. But he could look frantic, casting wildly about in case something had escaped him and gnawed by the fear that, for all his skill, he might have put his hand on the second rate when all the time the best was in another town or another country. His things had been got at risk. In every case the taking could not have been more difficult if it had been accompanied by thunderclaps. But he was not after ease. He had an eye for colour, but it was an anguished eye. He brooded on the notion that even colour might have escaped him—not just a shade, but some undiscovered primary colour which he might have missed through defective vision or simply because a human eye had serious limitations.

Pirie professed scorn at limits. But the difficulties of his secret trade had given him one overwhelming obsession. It was the wastefulness of the natural world which mystified and fascinated him. He felt unease at the superabundance, the spill-over of the earth's stuff. At times he felt fury. He had a puritan's fear of waste, and on a smaller scale, would no more have dreamt of going after things which were free for the taking than he would of bending to pick up those objects thrown up with savage lavishness on the shore in one night's storm. He wondered superstitiously what sort of backlash might come from a force which produced seeds, stars, animals and insects on this colossal scale. There were split seconds when, against such a background, he saw himself as mean to the point of deformity—flashes when, to his own eyes, he appeared bent double as though the furtive minutes of his life had been locked together in one permanent arthritic stoop. This malignant image would fade from his mind as quickly as it had come.

He made discoveries in his own field. Lately, he had found he could slice the costly leatherback from the end of a library shelf as neatly as he'd long ago lifted the folded napkins in a hotel lounge. He glanced into these books before he sold them—learnt scraps of old medicine and botany, bored himself blind over theological arguments which might once have startled his great-grandfather. There were things in his head which scholars in the subject had missed. He amused himself—but not for long—with travellers' tales, allowed himself to skim momentarily along the blue edges of icebergs or up tropical rivers against a steamy broth of fishes and strange vegetation. What he could not abide was fiction in any form. He knew it for what it was. Lies. He rifled through the classics, through new novels. Columns of conversation caught his eye. He frowned to see the characters turning themselves inside out and upside down to one another's view. He scanned a volume from first page to last to find one mention of the hero's job and was scandalized to reach the end no better informed. He jumped passages of love-making as across raging torrents, landing pages on in a new crowd, a new city, and immediately taking off again, skimming, jumping till he found a last landing-place on which to take his stand. And his standpoint never changed. There was nothing here for him, and there was nothing because it was lies, all lies from start to finish.

About this time he discovered one day, on the outskirts of the city, a secondhand bookshop which he hadn't known of before. It was not a place for rich bindings. While he hung about for a few minutes he accidentally knocked a pile of magazines from a stool and was setting them up again when the owner spoke from the back of the shop.

'Take them! Take the lot. You can have them for thirty pence.' It seemed more like a gift than a bargain.

'Thanks, no,' said Pirie, starting to pile them up again.

'What!' said the man.

'I don't want them.' Pirie spoke coldly, scarcely moving his lips. But he bent and picked a magazine off the pile, then slowly another, and another. It was a periodical on astronomy and each number had a coloured cover. On one was a whirlpooling, greenish galaxy, hurling off stars, on another a globular cluster, dense at its centre as a snowball; on another a blacked-out sun in eclipse, the corona frayed with scarlet loops and spirals; on another a blue nebula veil. Twelve in all. And on the last, set against black space, were the minute, tilted discs of distant galaxies. Pirie's heart had jumped at these sights. His shoulders remained rigid as he flipped through them.

'A good set,' said the man, watching him and flicking his duster over a table of books. 'A bit tattered. But the photos are magnificent.'

'I don't need them.' Pirie's voice was pitched thin and high.

'The photos *and* the text. Both excellent. The text is a bit out of date. That's the only reason they're going cheap. That and a few stains here and there.'

'Out of date?' Pirie turned his head and spoke with contempt. But it was for his own eagerness he felt the greatest scorn.

'By out of date,' said the man evenly, 'I mean not much more than fifteen years or so. But I'll admit a few years can bring out a hell of a lot of new kinks in the cosmos. Another ten might show the whole affair turned inside out. But look at your pictures! Will you ever see better?'

Pirie gathered up the journals awkwardly, dropped a

couple, gathered them up again and tried to pile them on the stool.

'Yes, that's how it is,' said the man coming forward. 'They'll clutter the place up, getting more tattered at every move. Twenty pence then. Take them or leave them.' As though conferring a particular favour Pirie took them.

For the rest of that day and well on into the night he went through the magazines. He sat first at his table, then at the fire, and finally on the floor, back to the wall. Once or twice he lay and stared up as though to pierce the plaster with his eyes. He had known about stars. He had made it his business years ago. But this lot burst without warning through everything he'd known before. Certain ideas had been blown to smithereens. With each page he turned the limits exploded further and further out. On the digits which stood for time and space the O's were multiplying like pond eggs in the sun.

Faced again with a shattering of confines Pirie reacted with the usual exhilaration and dread. But it went deeper than before. Next day, surrounded by magazines, he ate and drank with the stars. He stirred his tea on the verge of spinning galaxies and noted how stars and liquid swirled together. He explored vast outpourings and sank through appalling extinctions, brooded on the blazing growth of supergiants which had collapsed into dense seeds. While he finished supper he found, in the last number of the pile, one page uncut. He slit it quickly with the breadknife and a great, blunt-nosed comet whizzed into view. He stopped eating and brooded superstitiously on the comet. Why was *he* the first to see it? He turned back to earlier numbers and went slowly on with his meal, stopping now and then to read or hold a page up to examine the almost invisible double of a star. And the day after he

211

went through the pile again. By this time he'd got a grip on himself, cooled to the point of calm. After a week he was in control and his final conclusion was that once again he'd been sold short, and with only himself to blame. For he remembered he'd been warned. This was out-of-date information, tattered facts. He brooded over it for a day or two as he went about doing other jobs, and finally he could hardly bring himself to glance at the magazines. In their way they were now no better than fiction. They were not completely true and that was the end of it. Each day they grew more tattered as though his angry eyes were reducing them to trash, and at last came the day when they were tied and dumped outside in the waste-paper sack. He missed the turbulence and luminosity of the photos more than he'd thought possible. He was out of a whirlpool, and the ground he was on felt deadly flat. But he was no child, he said, to be placated with pictures if the rest was wrong.

Yet his mind ran more than ever on stars. One day, not many weeks after he'd dumped the magazines, he spotted a book on astronomy in the main bookshop of the city. The huge volume, heavy as a tablet of stone, had everything. Amongst the nine hundred pages of text were coloured photos as good and better than any he'd seen, diagrams and drawings by masters, with maps of the sky folded between the front and back covers. The book was written by experts and recommended by experts. It was full of the poetry and the mathematics of stars, and it was fresh from the publisher. Pirie knew what he'd found. There could be no question of making a grab for it. Bargaining was out. This was the pearl, and he would pay for it. He examined the £12 price ticket. He examined the publication date again to make sure of year and month, checked the corners of the book to see that it was perfect and rifled quickly through in case anyone had left a print on the new pages. There was no flaw in it. Finally, he opened the book in the centre and sniffed. The print smelt bitter and fresh at the same time. To Pirie it smelt of the blackness of outer space, but space confined. And now owned. For by a stroke of luck he had money enough in his pockets. He walked to the desk with the book under his arm and began to leaf out the seven single pounds and the five pound note. This he did with some arrogance, sharply rapping the side of his thumb down on top of each note as he flipped it out —as though each one, for the benefit of unbelievers, must be both seen and heard. There was a slight altercation over wrapping.

'It would be better to have it wrapped,' said the assistant.

'I'll take it as it is.'

'It is customary for books to leave our premises wrapped.'

'I'll take it as it is or not at all.'

The assistant nodded. Pirie left the desk with his un-wrapped book under his arm, and he took his time. There were a few people around. Nearby, a fat man who was lean-ing against a shelf of cookery books, reading recipes, smiled at Pirie as he went past. Pirie had made no study of smiles and had no clue to the meaning of this one. He paused, took the book from under his arm and ceremoniously un-folded the black and white star-map at the back, letting it hang over his elbow almost to the ground while he studied it. The fat man detached himself from the shelf. 'That's some book you've got there!' he murmured to the bent head. There was no response. Pirie had risked him-self more than most but he had an instinct that the spon-taneous word, friendly or hostile, might one day destroy him. The man took a couple of steps forward till he stood at Pirie's elbow. 'It seems we've a common interest,' he said. 'And that *is* a book! *That* one's a prize!' He touched the ruffled stream of stars with one finger.

'Yes!' said Pirie sharply.

'And you've wasted no time at all. It's as crisp from the press as a cake from the oven.'

'Yes!' Pirie quickly folded the map and closed the book. 'It's the last word.'

'The latest. Oh, of course!' said the fat man. 'Right up to the mark. *Not*, naturally, the last word.'

Pirie's heart jerked. He sensed a threat. He felt his limits strain and snap. 'The last word!' he said again, drawing his breath in sharply.

'We can't fool ourselves, can we?' said the fat man smiling. 'There *is* no last word. Can't be and never will be.'

Pirie was moving away but he turned his head to throw a cold, galled glare behind. 'Till next year then—the last word!' he said.

'Get along—you're joking!' the other replied. 'Not till next month or next week or tomorrow. The last word? Not even till the next split second!'

Pirie had reached the door but he turned again. 'What do you think I paid for?' he asked in his cold, clipped voice.

'To be always on the move—and in the dark,' said the fat man genially as Pirie stepped outside and started off down the street. 'To be aghast—endlessly!' he called after him. He stood for a minute watching Pirie, then came softly back and took up his stance at the shelf. Pirie was already two blocks away. On one side of him moved lines of cars. On the other, a jostling crowd. Shadows of chimneys, of awnings, trees and lamp-posts moved on the ground in front and behind. But these were not the only movements conspiring to unfix him. There was a vibration of

214

dust and light in the air, an endless drift of light and dark particles circling alone or in groups—so erratic, so devious, there was no knowing whether they belonged to his own eyes, to the outside world, or to both. Moving rapidly, but with the painful precision of a tightroper slung in the void, Pirie went along the uneven edges of the pavement, his eyes down.